Nelson's Curious Adventure

Cheryl Wright

Copyright

Nelson's Curious Adventure
(SANTA PAWS CHRISTMAS COZY MYSTERY)

Copyright ©2025 by Cheryl Wright

Small Town Romance Publications

This is a work of fiction. Characters, places, and incidents are a figment of the author's imagination. Any resemblance to actual events, locales, organizations or people living or dead, is totally coincidental.

- This book was written by a human and not Artificial Intelligence (A.I.).
- This book cannot be used to train Artificial Intelligence (A.I.).

Dedication

To our amazing senior dog, Bindy.
We love you dearly.
You are a very important member of our family,
and always will be.

To Margaret Tanner, my very dear friend and fellow author, for her enduring encouragement and friendship.

To Alan, my husband of over fifty years, who has been a relentless supporter of my writing and dreams for many years.

To You, my wonderful readers, who encourage me to continue writing these stories. It is such a joy knowing so many of you enjoy reading my stories as much as I love writing them for you.

Table of Contents

Chapter One

Early December – Present Time – Pleasant Valley, Montana

Being so close to Christmas, the store was hectic.

Jennie Carpenter glanced across to the other side of the room. Nelson was curled up where he always was – on his oversized bed.

He was the store mascot, and everyone loved him. His bed sat on a cupboard that divided the store from the café. Originally built for storage, it was now totally enclosed to ensure Nelson's safety. Jennie could see him from the front register, which suited her fine.

Everyone loved Nelson and inevitably reached out and petted the adorable puppy.

There was no doubt he was cute, and he certainly loved pets. And cuddles. He would take as many as he could get. Nelson particularly enjoyed seeing repeat visitors. It was as though he knew them intimately. Which of course was ridiculous.

Except it was a dog thing.

The bell over the door tinkled. Snow blew inside as the customer hurried inside. Jennie studied him, but only for a moment. This man was unknown to her. She strode the few steps it took to reach him. "Welcome," she said brightly. "I'm Jennie Carpenter. Owner of this little bookstore."

He looked her up and down, then smiled. "Aiden," he said, reaching out to shake her hand. "Aiden Philpott."

Jennie stared into his face. She hadn't seen this man before, but his name seemed familiar. She felt certain the reason would eventually come to her.

"You have a busy store here." His eyes landed on Nelson, and he smiled.

They both watched as an elderly woman reached over, and patted Nelson. She spoke gently to the pup, and he glanced up at her, a smile on his face and his little tail wagging. She picked Nelson up out of the enclosure, which was not allowed.

This was the first time anyone had picked him up. Hopefully it was the last. Apparently, the sign stating "Do not remove Nelson from his enclosure – for his safety" was not enough of a deterrent.

When the woman turned to face them, Jennie could see it was Mrs. Featherall. She waved to Jennie and Aiden, then smiled. "Nelson is so adorable," Mrs.

Featherall called across the room, then went back to petting and cuddling the nine-month-old pup.

Jennie smiled, then turned away. She loved Nelson with all her heart. But every time she looked at him, it reminded Jennie of what she'd lost.

The loss of Bridget Carpenter had hit Jennie hard. Her grandmother had opened the store more than two decades ago. It had quickly become a popular place for locals to stop by. Pop had been instrumental in fitting out the store exactly the way Grammy wanted. A small café was built as part of the bookshop. It was nothing fancy, and, with a few tweaks over the years, was still very functional.

In the beginning, the business was a one-person job, but as time went on her grandmother leased out the café. It was too much for her and turned out to be the best thing she'd done. The café had quickly drawn people into the store. From that moment onwards, sales of the books markedly increased.

It had not only become a place for locals to congregate. The store was busy enough to keep it afloat. It was especially true at particular times of the year—Mother's Day, Valentine's Day, and the busiest of them all, Christmas.

This was the first Christmas without Jennie's beloved Grammy. Her heart was broken. She had worked in the store, alongside her grandmother, for many years. The bookstore had become a second home to Jennie, as she knew it had been to her grandmother. She also knew it had become something of an institution to locals, but more than that, as the years rolled by, Grammy could no longer cope alone.

After Pop's death, her home of over fifty years felt lonely. It was then she decided to get a furry companion. Nelson's original owner could no longer look after him, and at four months he was placed in the shelter. Jennie went with her grandmother to find a suitable dog, and the moment the pair set eyes on Nelson, they knew he was the one.

They didn't even wait to make the decision, not that it was Jennie's to make. He was adorable, and those big brown eyes staring up at them meant there was no way the pair could leave without the delightful puppy.

Jennie hadn't seen Grammy so excited for a long time. It was a whole new venture for her, but she didn't want to leave the pup home alone during the day. In the end she made the decision to bring him to the store where she could keep an eye on him. Their bookstore customers were delighted. Mrs. Featherall was particularly happy to see Nelson. At first, she was confused, and thought he was her own dog, Misty. Jennie was aware the older woman's dog was a senior, not a young pup like Nelson.

She wasn't even convinced he was the same breed as Nelson, but she knew he was the same white color. Nonetheless, Nelson enjoyed the attention. When it all became too much, he glanced across the room at Jennie. That's exactly what he was doing right now.

She excused herself from her visitor and headed to the dog and the woman who held him tenderly. "I think he needs to go potty," Jennie told Mrs. Featherall. She took Nelson from the elderly woman's hands, then headed out the back and into the small garage where his litter tray was kept. Nelson did his business once they were there. At least he didn't have to go out into the icy snow.

"There you are," Mrs. Featherall called across the room as the pair returned. "I wondered where you'd gone."

Her customer's memory must be failing her, Jennie decided. It was only minutes ago Mrs. Featherall watched her take Nelson outside. Had confusion set in since the loss of her husband?

Perhaps it was part of the grieving process. Grammy had become forgetful after Pop had passed on. Jennie smiled and placed Nelson back in his bed. He loved the attention, and who was she to take that away from him?

Whenever it got too much for him, Jennie placed Nelson in his second bed, which was in an enclosure behind the counter, out of reach for customers. He clearly relished the attention, but also seemed to appreciate the peace and quiet sometimes.

Should she bring him behind the counter now? Did he seem overwhelmed? Jennie didn't think so, especially given he'd been outside, away from the flurry of the bookstore.

Mrs. Featherall appeared confused. "Where's Bridget?" she asked as she scrutinized each and every corner of the store.

Despite her own heart breaking, Jennie put a hand to the woman's shoulder. "Grammy passed on, Mrs. Featherall." Tears filled the other woman's eyes. Jennie led her the few steps to the small café and guided her into a chair. "Let me get you a pot of tea," she said gently.

The upset woman nodded.

"Mrs. Featherall is distressed about Grammy," she told Todd who leased the café.

"But…" He studied Jennie, and then Mrs. Featherall. "She attended the funeral," Todd finished.

"She seems quite confused today. A pot of tea is in order. On the house." Jennie glanced across the store and noticed several customers waiting to pay for their book purchases. She hurried over.

Grammy and Mrs. Featherall were friends for most of their lives. It cut Jennie to the core to see the elderly woman in such a state. Her heart hurt, but there was nothing she could do about it.

12

Chapter Two

Aiden glanced about. He'd only entered the store because of the sign on the window. The one that said café.

He'd been working hard and needed a break. And a coffee. This seemed like the perfect place. Until he stepped inside. It was far busier than he'd expected, and was noisy. He should have realized it would be that way. It was almost Christmas, after all.

For the first time, he noticed the wood fire on the other side of the room. It was in the café itself, and Aiden was certain it must draw a lot of customers in here. Especially on days like this.

He picked up one of the menus as he made his way to the café's counter. Coffee was all he really needed, but a snack would hit the spot. Except the menu didn't mention any snacks, cakes, or slices.

Aiden went up to the counter anyway.

"May I help you?" the worker asked. Todd was written on his name tag.

"Thank you, Todd," Aiden said moments after he spotted a glass cabinet full of baked goods. "A large cappuccino, and a small plate of mixed pastries, please." He glanced across the room to where Mrs. Featherall sat alone, drinking her tea. She looked so lonely, and completely lost. "I'll be with Mrs. Featherall," he said. "We'll be sharing."

Todd's grin lit up his face. "That's very kind of you," Todd said, then went about preparing Aiden's order.

Standing next to the table where the elderly woman sat, Aiden waited for her to acknowledge his presence. She slowly lifted her head and gazed at him. "Do I know you?" she asked, confusion on her face.

"We met some time ago," Aiden told her. "Plus, I was at the counter with Jennie when you were petting Nelson. Would you mind if I join you?"

She studied him for long minutes, then glanced about. Aiden was certain this was done with her safety in mind. With dozens of people wandering about the store, Mrs. Featherall seemed comfortable with the arrangement and indicated for him to sit down.

It wasn't long before Todd placed Aiden's coffee in front of him, and the mixed pastries in the middle of the table. He also left two small plates and napkins. After thanking the man, Aiden offered a pastry to his new companion.

"I didn't order anything," she told him, shaking her head. "Did I?" The dear lady certainly was confused. Jennie seemed worried, which made him concerned. Mrs. Featherall was around the same age as his grandma. He would hate to see her in such a state.

"Consider it a gift from me to you," he said gently. "Help yourself."

Clapping her hands with joy, the older woman reached out and took one of the pastries. Taking a dainty bite, she seemed to savor every bit of it.

Aiden reached for a pastry and did the same. They were melt in your mouth. This might be the first time he came here, but it certainly wouldn't be the last.

"Who are you?" Mrs. Featherall asked gently. Her eyes showed her confusion, and it bothered Aiden. He had first met her many years ago when he'd first visited Pleasant Valley. In her current state, he didn't expect Mrs. Featherall to remember. He did think she might remember their interactions only months before her husband passed.

He leaned closer to his companion. "Aiden Philpott," he told her softly. He could easily have added they'd spent significant time together over a number of days. When her husband was still alive.

Aiden might have reminded her she'd invited him to dinner on more than one occasion. Both she and her husband, Ron, insisted they get re-acquainted before any transactions took place. Ron had long retired, but had hired a young buck to run the business for him. Once he discovered his time was limited, he needed to finalize the details.

Aiden shook his head. Ron was a nice man. A kind man, and he had no doubt the townsfolk loved him. Stepping into his well-worn shoes was going to prove difficult.

"Oh, I think I do remember you," she said excitedly. "Did you take over my husband's business?"

Relief hit Aiden hard in the chest. He worried Mrs. Featherall might have Alzheimer's. But with her husband dying, add to that her best friend, her mind may be a little confused right now. It was highly possible.

"I did indeed," he answered, then offered her another pastry.

She reached out and took another pastry, once more savoring the deliciousness of it. Aiden wondered who made them. Was it Jennie? More likely Todd. He was the café manager, it seemed. Either way, he would certainly return some time soon.

His plan had been to settle here in Pleasant Valley sooner, but he'd had to finish out his contract in the city. That meant he needed to keep on the young buck Ron had employed.

By all accounts Ron wasn't necessarily happy with the man, otherwise, why plan to get rid of him? On the other hand, perhaps Ron simply wanted to finalize his business and related assets before his imminent death. Aiden couldn't blame the man for tying up loose ends so his wife wouldn't have the difficult task.

Mrs. Featherall drank down the last of her tea. Aiden drained his mug of coffee, then stood. "I will be leaving soon, Mrs. Featherall. Might I escort you home?"

She gazed at him questioningly. "You don't know where I live," she said. Then moments later added, "Do you?"

These were all classic signs of Alzheimer's, but she needed real testing, not just a diagnosis across a café table. It made him wonder if Jennie was aware of the dear lady's condition.

Aiden reached out a hand and helped Mrs. Featherall to her feet. "I do know where you live," he said gently. "I will see you home safely, if it's the last thing I do." He helped the elderly woman into her coat and waited for her to don her gloves, scarf and hat.

Once he was rugged up, too, he linked his arm through hers, and they walked through the bookstore and out onto the street.

Thankfully, it wasn't far, and Aiden would soon have this dear lady safely tucked away in her home. He wasn't happy leaving her there alone, but what choice did he have?

Chapter Three

Jennie barely had time to breathe, but she noticed the interaction between the stranger, Aiden, and Mrs. Featherall. He sat with her in the café, and they shared pastries, which was very kind of him.

She shuddered when the pair headed out the door together. She didn't know this man, and neither did Mrs. Featherall. Or did she? It wasn't like her to trust strangers. She was normally quite wary of people she didn't know.

Except today was no normal day. Today she was a bundle of confusion. It was then Jennie realized – it was six months today since Ron Featherall had passed. Anniversaries such as this were difficult. She knew this first-hand, since it was coming up to the two-month anniversary of Grammy's passing.

Her heart thudded. It had been a difficult year, there was no doubting it. In the months leading up to Grammy's passing, they'd discussed the store's future. Grammy was adamant it must stay in family hands.

Jennie had no intention of selling the store and had no clue why her grandmother would insist on such a condition. The pair had lived together for some years. Once it became apparent the older woman's health was failing, she no longer felt comfortable living alone. It seemed like a natural progression. Jennie had been working at the store for quite a few years by then. It was far too much for the frail woman, who was now in her late eighties.

Jennie's actions were motivated by love. For her grandmother, whom she adored, and the bookstore, as well.

She glanced across at Nelson. The puppy was her saving grace. Knowing Grammy wanted her to look after Nelson for the rest of his days brought warmth to her. There was no question, she had no thought of not keeping him. The Havanese pup was everything to Jennie, as he was to Grammy.

Nelson was part of the family. A huge part.

Warmth filled her whenever Jennie thought of the pup. She glanced across at him and saw the distress in his eyes. The store had even more customers than before. It was clear he was overwhelmed, and she needed to take action.

Jennie strolled over and picked him up. She held the sign telling customers Nelson loved pets but to refrain picking him up, and flipped it over. It now stated *Nelson needs a break. He'll be back soon.* He quickly settled into his second bed, the one behind the counter, and curled up, ready for sleep. Jennie checked he had plenty of water, along with kibble.

Nelson knew this was his safe place. He couldn't wander or get lost due to the enclosure he was in. He was only an arm's length from Jennie as she rang up book sales, wrapping them in holiday themed paper for those who requested it.

She glanced at her watch. Still another hour until the store closed. *Bound by Books* stayed open late in the weeks leading up to Christmas. Doing so accommodated those who worked late. It was a long-time practice, and one she had no intention of changing.

Suddenly there was a lull in activity. She slumped against the counter. The store was still busy, but the hustle and bustle was slowing, much to her relief. Jennie had thought about getting someone to help her for the Christmas rush but had done nothing about it.

There were plenty of trustworthy people in town who she was certain would welcome the work. Not to mention the additional money for Christmas. She promised herself she would make some phone calls first thing tomorrow.

Bound by Books had become a central hub in Pleasant Valley. The store's café was the place friends met for coffee, where families came for lunch, and there was even a book club which met here once a fortnight after coffee and cake.

The door suddenly opened taking all her attention. Heavy snow was forced in by the strong wind. Unexpectedly, Aiden stood there, his gaze seeking her out. Jennie's heart hammered. She'd worried about Mrs. Featherall going out with this stranger.

He strolled over to her at the counter. "I wanted to let you know Mrs. Featherall got home safely."

His words sounded truthful, but she was still wary. "Was she able to direct you?" Jennie asked, believing she would trip him up.

Aiden frowned. "I have visited there previously – before Ron passed on," he said, sounding more than a little confused. "Perhaps I should start over," he said gently. "I am Aiden Philpott. The new town doctor."

She was even more confused now. Doctor Ron Featherall had passed six months ago. The town had not been without a doctor all this time. It couldn't have. "How…?" She couldn't finish the sentence, her confusion stopped Jennie in her tracks.

"I see your confusion," he said. "I am new to town. Ron had a locum in place when I bought the business. I had a contract to fulfil in the city." He shrugged his shoulders. "I kept the locum on until I was able to take over, plus some time to learn the ropes."

The relief Jennie felt was profound. Aiden was not a stranger passing through. He was a resident of Pleasant Valley, and as the local doctor, was automatically deemed trustworthy.

He glanced across to the dog bed. "Where's Nelson?" he asked urgently.

It was nice to know he was looking out for the pup. "He's behind the counter. Sometimes he needs a break. It's far too busy in here tonight, and this is his tranquil hideaway."

Aiden's face relaxed. He seemed genuinely happy to know the puppy was safe. "About Mrs. Featherall," he said gently. "She seems rather confused. Is that normal for her?" he asked softly.

"Today is the six-month anniversary since she lost Ron."

"Ah," Aiden said, understanding dawning. "That could do it. Still, I'll keep an eye on her. I owe that much to Ron."

His statement confused Jennie. Why did he owe Ron anything? Hadn't he paid for the practice? It would normally be the way of things. As though he picked up on her confusion, he went on to explain.

"I trained under Ron decades ago. He taught me so much, more than I'd ever expected. He was a much-loved mentor. When he was ready to sell the practice, he contacted me." His eyes showed his sadness at his mentor's passing. "He already had a locum in place, but he was not interested in running his own practice."

"But you were." Jennie could see there was more to the story, but Aiden didn't add to what he'd already shared. Instead, he gazed at Nelson.

"He really is adorable," Aiden told her, then pulled off his coat and gloves. "Can I get you anything? Tea? Coffee? Eggnog?"

At first, she thought he was joking, but it quickly became evident he was deadly serious. "Tea would be wonderful," Jennie told him. "Todd knows how I have it."

Aiden nodded then headed to the café. It wasn't long before he returned.

Jennie took a sip of the hot beverage. She closed her eyes and savored every drop. "I really needed that, thank you."

He smiled, almost grinned, as though he had saved the world. "Might I walk you home when you're finished tonight?" he asked. "It's not safe out there for a woman alone."

She knew he was right, but didn't want to impose. Jennie was about to say as much when Aiden answered for her. "It is not an imposition. Not in any shape or form. It is an offer to ensure you get home safely. Not only in this awful weather, but in the dark."

Jennie gazed at him. He certainly seemed trustworthy, and he'd got Mrs. Featherall home safely. But… "You don't know where I live," she reasoned.

"Except I do. Mrs. Featherall pointed it out on our way home. Although she said it was Bridget's house. Bridget was your grandmother? She talked about her all the way home. And you."

Without warning, tears sprung to her eyes. Jennie turned and wiped them away, not wanting this stranger to see how affected she was by his words. Unfortunately, it didn't work.

"I'm sorry," he said softly. "I didn't mean to upset you."

"I know," she said, then looked to the floor. Nelson was there, rubbing his little body against her legs through the enclosure. Jennie reached down and lifted him into her arms. "He misses her, too," she whispered, rubbing her cheek against his face.

Aiden watched their interaction. "It's to be expected," he said gently. With those few words, Jennie immediately knew he, too, had a pet. Whether it was a cat or dog, she had no idea and would likely never find out.

Chapter Four

Aiden felt terrible. He didn't mean to upset Jennie. He'd learned from his elderly companion it hadn't been long since Bridget had passed.

They both missed her terribly.

Nelson had been Bridget's constant companion and had meant a lot to both Bridget and her granddaughter. He could see why. Nelson was a sweet boy. He enjoyed the company of others and lapped up the attention he attracted in the store.

Jennie was right to remove him from the center of activity when it became too much for him. Leaving him home alone all day was not an option. He was one who adored seeing his many friends, even if those friends weren't canines.

"Honestly," Jennie told him firmly, "you don't need to hang around. I make the short trip home alone every night."

Just because you can, doesn't mean you should. The words sat on his lips, but he didn't voice them. Jennie Carpenter was one of the most fiercely independent women he'd ever come across. Living in a small town was good, until it wasn't. "I have nothing else to do," he told her, not wanting to let her see he was worried about her safety.

She shrugged her shoulders. "If you're sure," she said, moments before another customer came to the counter with their purchases.

Aiden took the opportunity to wander about the store. It would be closing soon, and he was sure there would be plenty to see. Jennie had gone to a lot of trouble to decorate for the holidays, both inside and out.

The floor to ceiling window with the store name taking up much of the glass, was like a beacon to passersby. It was the reason he'd dropped in. Seeing the café with its happy patrons, and the image of a steaming hot coffee waiting for him was more than Aiden could resist. Especially on such cold night as this.

He walked around the store, acknowledging many of the customers. Some he'd met previously, others he was sure he would eventually get to know, but in a more professional capacity.

"Terrible weather we're having."

The words came from behind him, and Aiden wasn't even certain they were meant for him. He slowly turned and found himself face-to-face with one of his patients. "Mrs. Spence," he said, silently relieved he remembered this patient's name. He was still learning them, since he hadn't been here terribly long. "It isn't particularly nice, but it's indicative of the time of year. What would Christmas be without snow?"

She laughed and left him alone. Small towns were like this – everyone knew everyone else. Pleasant Valley was no different. Helena was the complete opposite. It was all hustle and bustle and no one knew anyone else unless they were related. He'd worked at the hospital's emergency room, and every patient was a stranger. Besides, he was always far too busy saving lives to get to know the person he was treating.

Leaving the city and moving to the quiet town of Pleasant Valley would be his new beginning.

When Ron Featherall rang him with an offer to good to refuse, Aiden had rushed to meet with him. The need was great on Ron's part. He was well past retirement age but had not wanted to pass on his practice to just anyone. In addition, his health had taken a turn for the worse.

The offer had come at a time when Aiden knew he needed to put the past behind him. To find a slower pace for his constantly busy life. He had already made the decision to takeover Ron's practice before he'd hung up the phone.

Moving here had been the best thing he'd done for a long time. He'd needed this. Craved it for so long, but his contract with the hospital said otherwise. Thankfully, Ron's locum was happy to stay on until Aiden could leave the city.

It still surprised him the locum didn't want to take over the practice himself. He'd been working for Ron Featherall for a number of years already. It had been clear talking to him, he was far more comfortable as a locum. Not having to worry about the business side of things was what kept him operating as a locum.

For Aiden, it was the exact opposite. He liked the control. The stability. He also liked the familiarity a small-town practice would bring to his life. He wouldn't be just the ER doctor anymore, the one who treated everyone's ailments.

Aiden reached out to a colorful book in the children's section. He had a niece who loved to read. If you could call it reading. Amy was three and a budding reader. The book now in Aiden's hands was a counting book. There were ducks, cows, sheep, and every barnyard animal you could think of. This book was perfect for Amy.

He continued to search the shelves of the children's book section. There was sure to be more books suitable for Amy's age group. He would get her some toys, of course, but she would be delighted with however many books he bought for her.

It had been brought to his attention many a time, by his sister, he spoiled Amy. His answer was always the same. *She's worth spoiling.* It always earned him the wrath of Amy's mother. Except they both knew it had become more of a game than an admonishment.

Out of all the things he missed about the city, and there weren't many, Amy was number one on his list. Her sweet smile, and her blonde curls got him every time. He would have to ensure he visited often, or risk breaking their bond.

Spotting a rack of small shopping baskets, Aiden snatched one up and placed the barnyard book in it. His eyes scanned the shelf, and finally fell on a book with textures. The front page had a picture of a sheep, with an oval of wool for its body. On opening the book, which was solid board, he found more textures inside.

From the gentle fur of a kitten to the rougher coat of a dog, as well as synthetic feathers, and more. This book was also placed in the basket.

"Oooh, I didn't know you had a little one, Doctor!" Mrs. Clarke said as she came up beside him.

Aiden was beginning to regret his decision to wander around the store, but knew Amy was going to enjoy these books for quite some time to come. "I don't," he said firmly. "They're for my three-year-old niece." Better to nip rumors in the bud before they had a chance to surface.

He'd been warned about the gossip that circulated in small towns, and Ron had cautioned him Pleasant Valley was no different. Once started, it's like wildfire, Ron insisted. He'd been grateful he didn't have to bother with it in the city.

"Lovely!" she said, briefly touching his shoulder, then hurried away.

Crisis averted. This time.

Aiden was still looking through the children's books when he realized the roar of customers chatting had become little more than a quiet whisper. He checked his watch, and discovered the store was about to close.

Placing this last book in his basket, Aiden knew he'd gone overboard but loved his niece. Besides, money was not a problem. She was worth whatever it cost to make her happy. He placed the picture book in his basket, only now noticing the basket was almost full.

Glancing up, he saw the place was empty except for himself, Jennie, and Todd. All the other customers were gone. Now he felt guilty. Asking Jennie to process his purchases after hours wasn't fair, but he desperately wanted these books for Amy.

He approached the front counter and heard a tiny bark. Nelson. It was the first time he'd heard the puppy bark, but over the noise of the chatter in the store, he wasn't surprised. With the quiet came the opportunity for Nelson to make himself heard.

It made Aiden chuckle.

"What's so funny?" Jennie wanted to know, a smile on her face.

Nelson barked again. He couldn't help but chuckle again. "Nelson barking. He is so quiet, but very cute." He lifted his basket onto the counter. "You can put these away for tomorrow if you prefer. I just don't want to miss out on them."

As she removed the books from the basket, Jennie's eyebrows rose. "You have a child? Good choices," she said, then began to ring them up.

Why did everyone assume he had a child? "I have a three-year-old niece. Amy," he said. "She adores books."

"They are perfect for her age, and Amy will love these. She'll read them over and over for many years to come. They are amongst our most popular children's books." Jennie wrapped each one individually in holiday paper, then placed them into a large reusable carry bag.

Aiden knew Amy would adore unwrapping each one. "I appreciate it," he said as he reached for his credit card.

"You get staff discount," she whispered, despite the store being empty except for the two of them and Todd.

"Oh no, please," he said, objecting to a discount of any kind. "I will pay full price like everyone else."

Despite his objection, Jennie still applied the discount, a grin on her face. "You are helping me, and Mrs. Featherall," she said, and finished processing his payment. "Time for a coffee before we leave, or do you need to rush off?"

"Coffee sounds good," he said, already looking forward to sitting down before their walk home in the blizzard-like weather.

Chapter Five

Jennie was exhausted. It had been a long day.

It was always like this so close to Christmas. She couldn't complain, it was good for business. She remembered the first year she worked with Grammy in the store. Back then, her job was only casual – she was there to help her grandmother with the store during the busy holiday season. She was happy to do it.

Sales were always elevated this time of year, and Grammy needed help. After a few years of helping out, it became clear her grandmother was struggling by herself. Not only in the store, but at home. It took some convincing, but finally Jennie managed to get Grammy to agree to Jennie moving in with her. By this time, she was already working full-time at Bound by Books. And loving every minute.

After ringing up Aiden's purchases and bagging them, she locked the front door. "Come on," she said firmly. "Time for a break." Together, they strolled into the café area, where Todd waited for their orders.

It wasn't long before he sat down with them, after distributing the drinks. He placed a plate of pastries in the middle of the table. "I know what you did for Mrs. Featherall," Todd told Aiden, studying him as he spoke. "It was very kind of you."

"She's a friend from way back," Aiden said, then lifted the coffee mug to his lips.

Jennie watched the interaction between the two men. Todd she'd known for many years. Though they'd only met a short while ago, Aiden felt like an old acquaintance to her.

As she sipped her coffee, Jennie heard a faint bark. Nelson. He was letting her know he wanted to join them. Jennie went to him. His sad little face asked the question – did you forget about me?

She couldn't help but chuckle. With her exhaustion, she did forget, and Jennie felt really bad about it.

She leaned down and picked him up. Nelson cuddled into her shoulder. They had a very special relationship. When Grammy was alive, he was definitely her boy. Now though, he and Jennie connected on a different level.

His little tongue came out and licked her hand. Jennie chuckled. It tickled. She patted the sweet boy as she carried him into the café. "Look who I found," she said joyfully. Time spent with Nelson was always enjoyable.

"He really is adorable," Aiden said, and reached out to pet the young dog. Nelson did not object.

Jennie watched as Aiden petted her puppy. "Do you have pets?" she asked, genuinely interested.

"As a matter of fact, I do," he said. "I have a chilled five-year-old Cavoodle. Molly is a trained therapy dog and works in the clinic by day."

Jennie couldn't help but smile. "What color is she?" She couldn't help herself. As a dog lover, she needed all the details.

Aiden chuckled. "Molly is the color of toffee, with a white heart on her chest."

Jennie closed her eyes for mere moments, picturing the sweet girl. "I hope to meet her one day."

"I'm sure that can be arranged," Aiden told her.

When she glanced across the table, Todd was smiling. He was watching the interaction between the two. "Todd is not a dog person," Jennie said, a grimace on her face.

"Hey!" Todd objected. "I love dogs, just not all the mess and hard work that goes with them." He chuckled then, trying to lighten the mood.

The three chatted until all the pastries were gone, and their mugs were empty. Nelson snuggled happily on Jennie's lap until he was disturbed.

After ensuring all the doors were locked, and the blind was down on the large window at the front of the store, they went their separate ways. Todd left for home, and Aiden accompanied Jennie and Nelson to their home.

Nelson was small enough to be carried, and that's exactly what Jennie did. But not before she rugged him up in his winter jacket. It wasn't Nelson's favorite thing to do, but it was icy outside. Jennie did not want to expose him to the elements, especially after being in the warmth of the bookstore.

"At least the wind has steadied," Aiden said. "It was almost like a Blizzard earlier."

They were both rugged up in their thick coats, warm scarves, gloves and beanies. Hopefully it didn't get any colder before they got home. Jennie couldn't wait to get inside and warm the house. She'd been gone practically the whole day and dreaded getting home this late in the holiday period.

They didn't talk much on the way, between the snow and the wind, it was almost impossible. Aiden unlocked the door for her when they arrived. With her hands full of Nelson, she appreciated it.

"I may see you tomorrow," Aiden said. "I'm not sure if I have enough books for Amy."

Jennie wasn't certain but thought he was joking. He'd already bought so many books for his niece, but one could never have too many books. Could they?

"Well, perhaps I'll see you then," she said in anticipation. A shiver ran down her spine. Jennie wasn't sure if it was from the cold or something else entirely. She just knew it wasn't something she normally did.

Aiden reached out and patted Nelson. The puppy did not object, just as he never objected in the store. He loved the attention. His little eyes glanced up at Aiden, almost begging him to keep going. Except he couldn't. It was getting late, and it was cold. Aiden had to go to his own home, and to Molly.

"Thank you for a wonderful evening," Aiden said, as he continued his attentions on Nelson. He then turned and walked away, huddling against the snow. Jennie felt bad that he'd come out here, in the snow and the wind and the cold, only to ensure she got home safely.

It wasn't like she hadn't done it before, because she did it every day. That said, she appreciated the thought, and the fact he'd insisted on accompanying her on such a bleak night.

Until recently, she would walk home with Grammy, and Nelson of course. All that had changed when Grammy had passed. As she lit the fire, and warmed the house, Jennie felt sad. She missed her grandmother so much. Tears filled her eyes, and Jennie wiped at them.

It hadn't been long, and she was allowed to grieve. She pulled Nelson to her and cuddled the pup. He did not complain.

~*~

It was a new day, hopefully not as cold. Less snow would also be helpful.

As she went about her work, these thoughts entered Jennie's mind. Of course it snowed at Christmas, it always did. There was nothing she could do about the weather. But she could make it more palatable for customers to come inside.

Todd had already lit the fire. It was burning well, and from the large window outside, it must look cozy here in the store. Nelson was snuggled up in his bed, but she knew it wouldn't be long before he'd be running around the store.

This time of day he normally took advantage of the empty store. Jennie glanced at her watch. Another half hour and the doors would be opened. In the meantime, she'd tidied the shelves, swept the floor, and did all the menial jobs that had to be done.

She glanced up to see Todd waving at her. She sighed in contentment. Her coffee was ready. He was a great guy, Todd, and Jennie appreciated him. Every morning, he had coffee for her, along with something for breakfast. It saved her time at home before she left for work.

She didn't complain, no matter what he served her it was always tasty. Todd baked everything himself, nothing was purchased from outside. They had a wonderful arrangement; she ran the store, and he ran the café. They were two separate entities, despite being in the one building.

When her grandmother had started the business and included the café, it was different. She tried to run them both, it was impossible. It wasn't long before she leased the café. Not only did it make her life easier, but the food was also far better. The greatest decision she made was to have a fully trained chef working the café.

Not only could the customers come in for books, but they could also sit and rest while they had a coffee and a pastry. Todd also accommodated those who wanted a light meal. This time of the year, it was the perfect situation. Sit down, drink, eat, and then shop. What was there not to like?

Chapter Six

Aiden sat at his large mahogany desk, pen in hand. He listened carefully, and wrote notes, as his patient outlined his issues. The man had ongoing health issues and needed careful reviews. He was still adjusting to having Aiden as his doctor. After consulting with Ron's locum for so long, the change had proven difficult for this patient.

George Smith was eighty-two. He did not adjust well to change, including this change of doctor. Even after two visits, the patient was still getting accustomed to being treated by Aiden instead of their previous doctor. Aiden stood and took Mr. Smith's blood pressure. It was still high despite medications. "Bear with me just a moment," Aiden told his patient. He then walked to the door and opened it. He glanced about the waiting room. It was now empty of patients.

Molly, his therapy dog, was in her bed. Aiden whistled softly, and Molly jumped up. It wasn't often she was allowed in the consulting room and was always excited at the prospect.

"Have you met Molly?" Aiden asked his elderly patient.

Mr. Smith glanced about the room, until his eyes landed on Molly. A smile came to the old man's face. The moment Molly saw him, she ran over. She was now in her glee.

The older man reached out a hand and petted the toffee colored cavoodle. His entire demeanor changed. His face relaxed, and he was filled with joy. Aiden took the older man's blood pressure again. Lower. Not low enough, but somewhat better.

Why Aiden hadn't thought of this before, he had no idea.

Perhaps it was because he was more concerned with the patient's health issues. George Smith was not in the best of health but was doing well for a man of his age. "She's a beauty," his patient said. "I lost my Coco not long after I lost my wife. It's been a difficult time," he said.

This was the most his patient had ever opened up to him. Which was exactly why Aiden had Molly. She didn't have to do much, but seemed to bring out the best in people. Whether that meant telling their doctor things they considered minor. Or the far bigger things that changed their lives forever.

"I'm very sorry to hear that Mr. Smith" Aiden said, and he truly was.

While he continued to pet Molly, the patient glanced across at Aiden. "It's been particularly difficult. Me and the missus were married nearly sixty years. Our dog Coco was a Bitsa – a bit of this and a bit of that," he explained. "He was my best friend." His eyes glistened with unshed tears. "He was with me for fourteen years." Aiden was now fully aware of what was really ailing his patient. It was grief, pure and simple.

"How long..." He began to ask.

The old man wiped away his tears. It hit Aiden right in the heart. "Nearly a year since I lost the missus, less since I lost the dog." He thought for a moment, before speaking again. "Might have been October," he said, sounding uncertain.

Either way life was challenging for George Smith. Short of suggesting he get another dog, there was little Aiden could do for this man. He would keep an eye on him, and ensure Molly was in the room for every visit. "Do you ever visit *Bound by Books*?" Aiden asked.

The old man rubbed a hand across his chin. "Not lately," he said. "Any reason I should? I don't always read books." He waved a hand in front of himself. "Do they still have that café? Used to be good. Me and the missus went there often. I haven't been able to bring myself to go there alone."

Finally, he was getting to the crux of the problem. Memories. They always cut right to the heart. Aiden knew exactly how that felt.

~*~

He walked out to the reception area with Mr. Smith. Aiden was concerned about his patient's state of mind. Molly had followed them out, and the elderly patient sat down and continued to pet her.

There was now a new dilemma for Aiden to try and solve. He wanted to tell his patient upfront get another dog. Except he knew that was not going to work. George Smith was grieving for both his dog and his wife. His physical illness was enough for him to deal with, but Aiden believed his grief was making it worse.

"Make an appointment for Mr. Smith for one week," he told his receptionist. She nodded and got to work. Ron Featherall did not have a receptionist. Neither did the locum, but he was only there to fill in for Ron. He had no control over whether there was a receptionist or not.

For Aiden it was imperative. He was happy to be with his patients, but not to deal with paperwork. Hannah was his receptionist, banker, and office manager all in one. That left Aiden free to see patients. He did not want to deal with all the red tape and paperwork that came with being a doctor.

As he stood by the reception desk, he couldn't help but watch the man and dog interact. It didn't take much to see this is what he'd been missing. If only Aidan could hand over Molly to George Smith for the short term. Except it was impossible. She needed to be here for other patients. On their next visit, he would suggest a dog for Mr. Smith.

He decided then and there, Molly would be relocated. From this moment forth, she would be in the consultation room. That way she was more accessible to patients. They could choose whether or not they interacted with his therapy dog.

Molly was not only good for his patients, but she was also good for him. What Aiden had experienced was traumatic. It might have happened a little over two years ago, but the heartbreak and the senselessness of it all would stay with him for the rest of his days.

"When is my next appointment?" Aidan asked Hannah.

By this time Mr. Smith had left. It was clear he'd been reluctant to leave. He had really taken to Molly. Perhaps Aiden, as his doctor, could arrange a visit to an animal shelter.

He knew exactly what it meant to lose someone close.

"Not until two o'clock," she told him. "That gives you more than an hour break."

Aiden preferred to be busy. Being idle, gave him time to think. Thinking sent his mind into a dark place. Seeing Mr. Smith in such a state of grief, did not help. Except it was his job to help the man, and that's exactly what he would do.

He leaned down and picked up Molly's bed and her toys, then moved them into the consulting room. This made more sense. Why he hadn't thought about this before, Aiden had no idea. Now that he thought about it, it made perfect sense to have her on hand when needed. If someone was allergic to dogs, she would be taken out.

"It's a great idea," Hannah said. "Did you see how much Mr. Smith perked up while petting Molly?"

Aiden smiled. "I certainly did," he said. Then returned to the consulting room to work out where he was going to place Molly's bed.

Chapter Seven

Jennie sat back after finishing her breakfast and coffee. She glanced across the table at Todd. "Thank you for another wonderful meal," Jennie said. "I look forward to this every morning. Now I have to work." She rolled her eyes. It wasn't that she didn't want to go to work, it was so comfortable here, near the roaring fire, she didn't want to leave. She stood, took the last sip of her coffee, then placed the empty mug on the table.

"You are always welcome," Todd said as he reached for the soiled dishes. "Enjoy your day," he said.

"You, too," Jennie told him. She reached down and picked up Nelson, he was curled up on the hearth. If there was warmth, Nelson was right there. The pair went out into the shop, and Jennie gently placed him in his bed.

Now it was time to start working. The blind was still down on the window and the door, as it should be at this hour of the day. She swept the floors then walked through the store, straightening bookshelves, refilling them where necessary, and getting everything ready for the day's customers.

Jennie instinctively knew it was going to be another busy day.

She checked her bag supply, checked she had plenty of change in the register, enough gift certificates, then went out the back to the storeroom. Her eyes roamed over the boxes of books stored there. This time of year, she always had plenty of additional stock. Especially children's books.

Last of all she went to the bathroom and freshened up. Jennie made certain her hair was still in place and added pale lipstick to her lips. She glanced at herself in the mirror.

She didn't look too bad, for now anyway. Most days leading up to Christmas were frantic. It was like this every year, and she should be used to it by now.

She glanced at her watch – less than a minute to opening time. Jennie hurried from the back of the store to the front. As she arrived Todd was opening the large blind on the full-length window. Jennie did the same on the front door. She was surprised to see a half dozen customers lined up waiting to come in.

Opening the door quickly, she ushered them in out of the cold. "Warm yourselves by the fire," she told the customers. They were all locals and knew where they needed to go.

As they headed inside, Jennie had a terrible feeling. For some unknown reason, she was certain today was going to be stressful. She hoped she was wrong.

Jennie sat behind the counter on the tall stool she had purchased for that reason. She figured she might as well rest while she could. Things could change at any moment. While her first customers of the day warmed themselves by the fire with a mug of coffee, Jennie took the time to do nothing.

It was a rare thing, and she knew from experience it wouldn't last. As if thinking it made it come true, the door opened. A cold draft of air and snow followed. Jennie glanced up. Her heart fluttered at seeing the person standing there. She hadn't expected to see Aiden this early in the day. He headed directly for her.

"No patients today?" she asked.

Aiden smiled. Jennie didn't know if that smile was for her, or something else had caused it. "I have a late start today," he said, then hurried over to Nelson. He stood in front of the dog bed and petted him. It was very clear that Aidan was an animal lover. He glanced at her over his shoulder. "I have a question for you," he said. "Is there an animal shelter here in town?"

As Aiden stayed with Nelson, and seemingly having no thought of leaving him, Jennie rummaged through the drawers of the desk. "I have a card here somewhere. Just give me a minute." He seemed more than happy to comply. Nelson wasn't complaining either. "Oh, here it is," Jennie said. "Are you looking for a dog?" It confused her because Jennie already knew he had a dog. Molly the Cavoodle.

He shook his head. "Not for me, but for one of my patients. I was hoping they would have a senior dog this patient could adopt."

Warmth flooded her. That Aiden would help a patient in this way, filled her with joy. "Senior dogs are the hardest to get adopted," she said.

Jennie knew it was true. Nonetheless, she hoped Aiden was able to find a suitable dog for his patient. She figured the patient was also elderly but knew better than to ask. Although she had to admit to herself, she probably knew who it was.

She walked across the room and handed him the card. "You could ring ahead and ask if you wanted to save yourself going out in the cold," she told him. "I assume you do have a car? The shelter is on the edge of town, and a bit far to walk in this weather."

He took the card and thanked her, and confirmed he did indeed have a car. Aiden glanced down at his watch. "I'll have to get moving if I'm going to get there and have time to look around before my first patient arrives." He stood then and glanced down at

Nelson. "Sorry boy", he told the pup. "I have work to do but I'll come back later."

He headed for the front door again. He turned back to face Jennie, a look of regret on his face. Why that would be, she had no idea, but it described her feelings exactly. Aiden put on his heavy coat, his gloves and scarf, along with his beanie. Then he stepped outside. The snow was heavier today and would get worse as Christmas approached. It was not the best time to be wandering around town. Still, Aiden had a job to do, just as Jennie did.

Why she felt sadness at his leaving, Jennie did not know. Nelson stared at the door. It was clear he'd taken to the new doctor, just as Jennie had.

~*~

The day flew by, which was typical on hectic days at the store. Jennie wasn't complaining, she liked it this way. It was far better than the days that dragged out when it was quiet. The shelves needed restocking, and she needed to get more bags from the storeroom.

Jennie glanced about. Nelson was snuggled up in his bed, and the customers we're checking out books. This had to have been the busiest holiday season the store had ever experienced.

"Hello dear!" Mrs. Featherall called from across the room as she waved. She was petting Nelson, which was not uncommon. Sometimes Jennie thought she may come here simply to spend time with Nelson. It made no sense really, since she had her own dog at home.

Mrs. Featherall's dog was much older, and it was possible he did not like the attention the way Nelson did. Apart from that, Jennie knew the older lady craved company. She often caught up with friends at the café, and that wasn't a bad thing. As a recent widow, she was surely feeling lonely.

Jennie waved back. "How are you today?" she asked as she headed out to the storeroom. "I'll be back momentarily; I just have to collect some stock."

Mrs. Featherall nodded, then turned her attention back to Nelson.

As she rummaged about the storeroom, finding the supply she needed, Jennie knew Nelson was safe without her in the room. Todd would keep an eye out for him anyway, which was reassuring. She pulled out three each of the children's books she knew were in low supply on the shelves. Would she have enough of each to get through this season? Grammy had always done the ordering, although Jennie had sometimes helped.

Doing the job alone, was totally different to watching over someone's shoulder. Sure, she often gave input, but now she had sole responsibility over what books came into the store. As her grandmother had told her many times, you are always learning. She assured Jennie, it would become easier with practice.

 If this year was anything to go by, she needed a lot more practice. The store had been open more than two decades, and this was her first time navigating the holiday season alone. Surely no one would judge Jennie on her first solo attempt?

She could only hope that was the case. Jennie hurried back into the store, not wanting to leave customers waiting to pay for their purchases. As it happened, the customers were still rallying around the books. It gave her the time to place the bags behind the counter. She placed the books on the front counter and sorted them in order of how they were on the shelves.

Jennie glanced across the room at Nelson's bed. Her heart thudded when all she saw was an empty dog bed.

Jennie tried not to panic. Where was Nelson? She looked for Mrs. Featherall but could not see her either. Had she been here, Mrs. Featherall would know where to find Nelson, Jennie was certain.

As her heart thudded, she checked the dog bed behind the counter. Nelson wasn't there either.

Now she really was beginning to panic. She ran to the fire in the café, because that was one of Nelson's favorite places on a chilly day like today. He was right there, in his bed when she went out to the storeroom, so he couldn't be far away. He was even there when Aiden was leaving. And that wasn't long ago, either.

She put her hand to her heart, trying to make it slow down, but of course that didn't work. Feeling defeated, she walked into the café and sat down. Todd hurried over. "What's wrong?" he asked urgently.

Jennie took a deep breath then let it out slowly. "It's... It's Nelson," she said. He's missing. I can't find him anywhere.

Todd studied her. Did he think she was making it up? "Where have you looked?" he asked gently. Many people have been petting him today. Maybe one of them picked him up and took him with them while they looked for books."

His words made her feel better. She hadn't looked where the books were kept, not believing for one moment anyone would take him into that area. Food and drinks were not allowed, so why would you think a dog would be allowed?

Jennie jumped up from the table, not waiting to find out if Todd had anything else to say. She was anxious to find her puppy. Her grandmother would be so upset if this had happened while she was still here. Jennie shook her head, she couldn't let her imagination run away with her. She hurried to the bookshelves, going from one to the other. Distressingly, there was no sign of Nelson.

At that moment it hit her. Perhaps he needed to go potty, and somebody took it upon themselves to take him outside. She ran out the back to the garage. She opened the door, but there was no one there. No person, and no Nelson.

It was enough to make her cry, and it almost did. The only thing that stopped her was Grammy's voice in her head telling her to keep her wits about her. That Nelson couldn't have gone too far.

Perhaps he snuck out between someone's legs when they opened the door to leave? There were so many possibilities, and Jennie was certain it had to be an accident. After all who would steal a small puppy on purpose? Especially one that meant so much to her?

Chapter Eight

Aiden had just enough time to warm up by the fire, have a light lunch and coffee before he had to start back at the clinic.

His visit to the animal shelter earlier in the day had been worthwhile. As he'd walked down the aisles, Aiden noticed how clean the pens were. Each dog had its own bed, with clean bedding, and a bowl of fresh water.

Many of the shelters he'd visited in the past were not pristine like this one. He'd glanced at the information displayed about each dog. He anticipated a small to medium sized dog, but not a young dog. For George Smith, he believed a senior dog would suit him best. Aiden had long believed dogs should not outlive their owners.

It was cruelty at its worst.

George had a few good years left in him, so a dog with similar prospects would be ideal. Aiden pulled out his phone and photographed a handful of dogs he considered good matches. He'd spoken to the staff, who had passed on their recommendations.

Now all he had to do was get his patient to agree.

He drank down the last mouthful of his coffee, Aiden savored it. He was enjoying the heat from the fire, but knew he would have to leave soon and go back out into the cold. He glanced at his watch—he had a few more minutes and would prefer to stay right where he was. However, it was not an option. His afternoon session was a busy one, and it would not do to be late.

Todd hurried over to his table. "I hope your meal was to your satisfaction," Todd said as he stacked the soiled dishes.

Aiden sighed. "It was delicious. I wish I could stay longer," he said. "I have a full list this afternoon, so it's not possible." He glanced out the window at the snow and the wind and shivered. Moments later he stood, knowing it was time. It wouldn't take long to get back to the clinic, mere minutes, but that's all it took for the icy weather to chill you to the bone.

He allowed time to pet Nelson before he left, but Nelson was not in his bed Perhaps Jennie had taken him outside to potty. The little guy was adorable, and Aiden fell in love with the puppy almost the moment he met him.

He hurried out of the café, grabbing his coat, scarf, and gloves as he went. Aiden opened the door, and dashed outside, putting on his beanie as he went. He glanced back momentarily but neither Jennie nor

Nelson were in sight. He didn't have time to wait around, or he would be late.

He braced himself as he stepped out onto the snowy sidewalk. He was used to snow where he came from, but the cold here chilled you to the bone. Aidan wondered if he would ever get used to it.

"Brrrrr," he said as he entered the medical clinic just a few minutes later. "That's something I wish I hadn't needed to do," he told Hannah, his receptionist. He stomped his feet just inside the door to ensure all the snow was gone. It wouldn't do to walk snow through the waiting room. It could then become a fall hazard.

His elderly patients already had enough to deal with, without having to worry about falls. Especially at the doctor's office.

Aiden glanced about. The waiting room was empty. For now, anyway. He walked behind the reception desk and glanced at the list of patients for the afternoon. He noticed George Smith on the list, which surprised him. His appointment was for later in the day. It was a good opportunity for Aiden to talk to him about getting a senior dog.

He hadn't met some of the patients scheduled for today, and he was eager to meet them. He hoped they felt the same. Aiden stood behind the reception desk longer than he should have. "I might have to get myself one of these heaters," he told Hannah. "I don't want to move from here, but I know I must."

Hannah glanced up at him and smiled. "It certainly is cozy. Better than being outside in the cold."

"Can you order one of those for me, only larger? We need to keep the patients warm, too." Aiden went into the consulting room with his list of patients and opened the file for the first patient he was to see today. It was difficult being the new doctor in town. Especially when the previous doctor had been here for so long. With the majority of his patients being elderly, it was even more difficult. He had already encountered several patients who were not coping with the change.

Glancing at his watch, Aiden knew his first patient should be here now. He went to the door and opened it. "Mrs. Baker," he called. A woman glanced up. She looked annoyed, as she had been talking to someone sitting nearby. She stood, then turned to the other woman. "I have to go," she said. "We can catch up again tomorrow at the bookstore."

The more he heard, the more Aiden realized the bookstore and café were the center point of this town. He had met more people there than anywhere else. That wasn't necessarily a bad thing, but he was just beginning to put the pieces together.

He hoped that meant his transition as town doctor would be smoother as a result.

~*~

It had been a long day, and Aiden was ready for it to end. He had one more patient to see, and that was George Smith. He braced himself for the conversation he wanted to have with the elderly man.

He glanced over the file for this patient, familiarizing himself once again with his health issues. Except Aiden knew it wasn't only his health that was affecting him. Grief and loss were a big part of his problems. He couldn't bring back the man's wife or his dog, but perhaps he could help him by suggesting a senior dog.

He took a deep breath and opened the door. "Mr. Smith," he said. George Smith was the only patient left in the waiting room and stood as quickly as possible for a man of his age. "Take your time, don't hurry," Aiden told him with a smile.

"I'm coming, Doc," Mr. Smith said. Then shuffled over to Aiden. He followed the doctor into the room and sat down. Molly immediately came to him, and the patient's demeanor instantly changed. It was then Aiden knew he was doing the right thing suggesting a senior dog for George Smith. He opened his mouth to say that very thing when his patient took him by surprise. "I've been thinking,

Doc," he said as he petted Molly. "Your girl here, had me thinking. I might want to get another dog, only not a pup, that would be too much."

Aiden couldn't believe what he was hearing. "It's interesting you should say that," he said gently. "I've been doing some research, and I thought..." He watched the patient carefully, trying to gauge his reaction, but the man's expression did not change. "How do you feel about taking on a senior dog?" It felt as though he'd blurted it out, but what else was he to do?

Mr. Smith smiled, and happiness filled his face. "You must be reading my mind. That's exactly what I was thinking. I couldn't cope with a puppy these days, although I've done it many times before. But a senior dog, that sounds perfect."

They then discussed some of the dogs Aiden had seen at the shelter. Interestingly, Mr. Smith did not question how he came about this information. He did, however, agree to visit so he could meet these dogs, and make a decision.

He knew he shouldn't, because he would be setting a precedence, but Aiden offered to take Mr. Smith to the animal shelter. He didn't know if his patient had a car, or even a license. By going with him, Aiden could help ensure he chose a suitable dog. One that wouldn't be a hazard to him.

Chapter Nine

It was late in the afternoon, and by this time Jennie was frantic. She couldn't leave the store to try and find Nelson, as there were too many customers. She admonished herself for not doing what she'd promised—securing someone to work in the store with her.

She sat at the counter and contemplated what to do next. She glanced at her watch; it was close to closing time. She never used her cell phone during work hours, but today was an exception. She thought about calling the police but decided she would become a laughing stock. Kidnapping dogs was not a crime.

Or was it?

"Philpott."

Aiden's voice came through clearly. Jennie didn't speak for a few beats. She wasn't sure what to say. Once she did, it all came out in a hurry. "Nelson's gone," she said quickly. "I don't know if he's been kidnapped, got out the door, someone stole him..."

"Take a breath. Calm yourself down," Aiden told her gently. "He couldn't just disappear. Somebody had to be involved. Are you sure he's not just hiding in the store somewhere?"

Jennie's heart thudded. "He's not here," she snapped. This was not like her, Jennie never lost her cool. But today was different—Nelson was gone, and she may never get him back.

She could hear Aiden breathing on the other end of the line, but he didn't say a word. Not immediately. "Are you still there? Jennie?"

Tears now filled her eyes. She had held herself in check for so long, but now emotion had taken over. Her cheeks were wet with tears. Rather than admit how upset she was, Jennie hung up.

Finally, it was time. She could lock the door—all the customers were gone, and it was the end of the business day. Only Jennie and Todd remained. As she wiped her eyes with a tissue, she heard shuffling of feet. When she looked up, Todd stood in front of her.

"I'm worried, too," Todd told her. He reached across and held her hand. "We'll work this out," he said. "Someone knows where Nelson is. It's probably all a big misunderstanding. He's got under someone's feet and run outside." He squeezed her hand. "Come on, I'll make you a coffee." He let go of her hand, and Jennie started walking around the counter, and toward the café.

It was then she heard pounding on the door. They hadn't yet put the blinds down, so she could see it was Aiden. His face showed his concern, and she felt bad. She had hung up abruptly rather than let him know how upset she was.

Seeing him stand there made her emotional all over again. Tears streamed down her face. Jennie was so angry with herself, how could she find Nelson if she was a sobbing mess?

"Open the door," Aiden shouted urgently.

It was her fault he was agitated. He could see her crying. Jennie reached for the door handle with shaking hands and unlocked the door. Todd stood nearby, ever her friend, and her support. She wiped her face again, feeling more embarrassed than she ever thought possible.

The moment he came inside, Aiden opened his arms to her. Jennie instinctively leaned into him. They did not know each other well, but they seem to have some sort of... She wasn't sure what it was. Friendship at the very least. Except Jennie knew it was already more than that. They had a special connection.

"I'll make coffee," Todd said, then walked away toward the café. He sounded a little annoyed, and Jennie wondered why. He had been fine only moments ago, but that was before Aiden arrived.

Aiden held her tightly, his hands rubbing circles over her back. "We'll find him," he said, and as much as she thought it was impossible, Jennie somehow believed him.

She glanced up at the man who was comforting her. She wasn't sure she could even talk she was so upset. "I hope so," she whispered. "I promised my grandmother."

He interrupted before she could finish the sentence. "I promise you, we *will* find Nelson." Aiden's voice was so sincere, and so adamant, how could she not believe him?

"As the store is now empty, except for the three of us, we should spread out and search every nook and cranny." What Aiden said made sense. With the store packed with customers, it was impossible to search thoroughly.

They each took a separate area, with Aiden volunteering to check the outside of the store. She'd already done that, but it did not deter Aiden, not one little bit. He went out to the storeroom first, then opened the back door. He wandered around outside for a few minutes, all the time Jennie held her breath. She should have been doing her search, but was convinced Nelson had escaped somehow.

"There's nothing here," Aiden said. "I was hoping to see little footprints going through the snow. I would have followed them if they had."

Jennie didn't know what to say. She was afraid if she said anything she might burst into tears again, and that was not going to happen. The best thing she could do for Nelson was to keep a cool head. She silently apologized to her deceased grandmother. After all, she would be watching all of this, Jennie was certain.

It was then Jennie believed her grandmother spoke to her from beyond the grave. *You're doing fine. Nelson is safe. You just need to find him and bring him back home.*

Jennie shook herself mentally, this couldn't be happening. It was all in her imagination. Stress would do that to a person. Instead of dwelling on it, Jennie went to her search area. She went in and out each of the bookshelf areas. She had done this before, and felt as though it was a useless exercise, but it was standing room only the last time she checked.

Thinking back on it now, Nelson could have been tucked away in any of those large bags some of those women brought with them. But who would do that? Most of the customers who came here, were regulars. Everyone loved Nelson. They all stopped to talk to him as they came in the door, and they petted him. It was something everyone did almost since the moment he became the store mascot.

Her grandmother did not want to leave Nelson at home alone during the day. Everyone agreed—dogs need company. They are very sociable creatures, and Nelson was certainly like that.

Why was she thinking in the past tense? The very thought distressed Jennie. She tried to get the thoughts out of her mind and continued to search, but it was useless. The puppy was not here. And she was certain this search would prove fruitless.

There was no doubt in Jennie's mind somebody had taken the dear boy. Emotion threatened to overtake her again, but Jennie fought it with all the strength she had left in her. If she fell apart, she wouldn't be able to continue. And that would result in not finding Nelson.

At that moment she heard the front door close. She hurried out and saw Todd looking around in the café. He was behind the counter, checking in the kitchen. He shook his head Nelson was not there either.

Moments later the front door opened again. Snow blew inside, and Aiden was not far behind. He slammed the door quickly and pounded his feet on the mat. He shook his head, and Jennie's heart broke.

Would she ever get to see Nelson again? Or hold him close to her heart? It was looking very much like it would not happen. She couldn't bear the thought of never seeing the puppy again.

"He's not there," Aiden said. "Whoever took him must have picked Nelson up and carried him." Aiden looked as defeated as Jennie felt.

Chapter Ten

The three of them sat at the table in the café. Aiden felt useless. He glanced across at Jennie—distress was written all over her face. It was now clear someone, whoever that someone may be, had taken the puppy.

Sitting around the table today, drinking coffee, was so different to the last time they'd done this. Previously, they were all happy. Nothing was amiss as it was now.

Aiden wracked his brain. Why would anyone do such a thing?

Everyone knew Nelson was Bridget's dog. And yes, he was Jennie's now, but that didn't alter the fact Bridget was the one who originally adopted him. She was such a well-loved person in the town, and it made no sense for anyone to do this.

Kidnapping a dog was a very strange thing to do. It was even more remarkable because it happened in broad daylight. The store was packed according to Jennie and Todd, and Aiden had no reason to question it. The Christmas season was always busy, they said. So much so, Jennie already had a problem remembering who had been in today. Most people paid by credit card these days, which meant it was no longer helpful with everything being electronic.

"Perhaps you could write down the names you remember," he told her. "It might lead to important information. You never know." Except Aiden was certain he did know. From what he'd seen in his short time in the store, no one took notice of anyone else. They were all focused on what they were doing. And that was choosing gifts for family and friends. It felt like they were fighting a losing battle before they even began.

Jennie jumped up from the table and hurried over to the counter. She was back in no time with a notepad and pen in hand. She started writing almost immediately and had listed around a dozen names before she stopped. "I can't think of any others," she said, her voice breaking.

Did she think this was her fault? It should be the last thing on her mind. She was a caring dog mom, and no one could deny it. It seemed to Aiden, Jennie cared for Nelson the same way a mother would care for its child.

"It will come to you," he said. "Perhaps not right now, but eventually." He reached across and put his hand over Jennie's. Aiden wondered if he was overstepping. She didn't pull her hand away, didn't even move, so he figured he hadn't. Jennie didn't seem to be the sort to withhold her feelings. If she didn't want him to touch her, Aiden was certain she would say so.

Aidens felt eyes on him. When he glanced up, Todd was staring at him. His eyes went from Aiden's face to his hand covering Jennie's. Was this Todd's way of admonishing him for his actions? No matter it wasn't Todd's business. If Jennie wanted him to move his hand, she would have said so. Or pulled her hand away.

This was nothing more than him trying to comfort the woman. His new friend. Except it was clear to Aiden he had become more than a friend to her. And he felt the same way. Otherwise, he would not have held her in his arms, he was certain of it.

"Have you got Mrs. Spence on there?" Todd asked. "She was in the café today, so I know she was here."

Aiden peered across at him. He hadn't even considered that angle but knew he should have. Many of the customers started in the café with a group of friends, or did their shopping first then gravitated to the café. It was almost a package deal for most people.

"I almost forgot," Todd said. "Mrs. Green was here today, along with her daughter Marion. There was also..." He closed his eyes momentarily while he thought. "Table ten," he said. "I've never seen them before. It was an older couple. They may have been from out of town, I don't think they were locals."

Jennie scribbled down the names Todd had given her and was poised ready for more. "Do you write down the names on your order pad?" she wanted to know.

Todd frowned. He reached into the pocket of his apron. "Indeed, I do," he said flipping through small notepad.

Aiden's heart pounded, not that Nelson was his dog, but he felt a connection. He could imagine how Jennie was feeling right now. If Molly went missing, he would be feeling the same way. At least he would have limited suspects if she did. He shook himself mentally; he had to put his focus back on Nelson's disappearance.

"Are you ready?" Todd wanted to know.

Jennie's hands were shaking. Aiden wasn't certain she would be able to write anything down. He took the pen and paper from her and nodded at Todd.

"Right," Todd said. "Let me know if I go too fast." He took a deep breath and then started reeling off names. "Mrs. Cowden, Mrs. Brown, Lily and Frank Rowlands, Birdie Garrett, Lizzie Driver, Mrs. Reed, Mary Mooney." He looked up from the pad momentarily. "I have plenty more if you want them, he said.

Instead of getting Todd to read them out Aiden suggested he take the pad and go through it alone.

He was worried Todd might take offence since he was already annoyed with Aiden because he'd held Jennie's hand. But he seemed fine and offered to get them coffee.

As Aiden had written down the names, he realized exactly how busy the store had been. He underestimated how many people went through the bookstore on a daily basis. It proved to him that Jennie really did need help. Todd could not help as he had his own business to attend to. It was now clear to Aiden, the café was every bit as busy as the bookstore. He turned to Jennie and smiled. "This is a big help. Not many cafés use this system with names. Most only use table numbers."

Jennie nodded. Aiden was certain that was all she was capable of at this very moment. He couldn't blame her. No one could. Finding Nelson would be a case of elimination, but they must concentrate on finding him.

It felt as though they had been planning for hours, and they had. Aiden realized there was nothing more they could do here and offered to take Jennie home.

She stared at him, her eyes glistening. "I... I can't leave, what if he turns up?"

They both knew that was not going to happen. Not tonight anyway.

Todd reached for the soiled dishes and glanced at Aiden before turning his gaze to Jennie. "I will ensure the place is locked up," he told Jennie. "There is nothing more you can do here. Go home, get some sleep, and come back fresh in the morning."

Aiden knew he was right, and was sure Jennie did, too. He stood and Jennie followed his lead. He hurried to the front door before she could change her mind. He reached for her coat and helped her into it. She didn't complain, but Aiden knew she was not thrilled. They both knew Nelson would not be back tonight.

The trouble was, they didn't know if the puppy was safe.

Chapter Eleven

Aiden walked her home in silence. They both knew she may never get Nelson back. Why anyone would want to take the puppy, Jennie did not know.

It surely had to be a mistake. Why would someone take a dog that was clearly not theirs? Her mind took her in all sorts of directions, Jennie needed it to stop. Now they stood outside her front door, and she rummaged through her bag looking for her house keys. Her hand shook so badly, she couldn't get the keys in the door.

Aiden's hands covered hers. The shaking stopped, and she felt comforted. "Let me," he said. He opened the door wide enough for her to get inside without the snow getting in, and she hurried inside. Jennie gestured for Aiden to join her, but he seemed reluctant.

That is, until he glanced at the empty fireplace. "There's something romantic about a fireplace," he said quietly.

Jennie knew he was right. But that wasn't the reason she used it. She could easily have had central heating installed, but this was the home of her grandparents, and she didn't want to change anything in it. It was a beautiful old house, more than enough for one person.

But now, it felt empty. She glanced across at the empty dog bed, and her heart broke all over again. She didn't say a word, she didn't have to. It seemed that Aiden knew exactly what she was thinking.

He studied her, his eyes sad. "I can't say I know how you feel," he said. "But I do know how I would feel if Molly went missing."

She glanced at him. "Molly?"

He looked surprised, then smiled. "Of course, you haven't met Molly yet. She's my therapy dog." He rubbed a hand along his chin. "I should say she's *a* therapy dog. Molly is there for my patients."

Jennie smiled. Just the thought of having a therapy dog at the doctor's office made her happy. "Oh! Now I know why you asked about the animal shelter. Your Molly convinced one of your patients they needed a dog."

Aiden grinned. "I can neither confirm nor deny," he said, still grinning. "What I can say is, Molly can be very persuasive."

After removing his coat, Aiden squatted down in front of the fire, reached for some logs and kindling, and screwed up some newspaper. Jennie was mesmerized watching him. He grabbed the matches from the shelf and lit the newspaper. She watched the muscles in his back as they contracted with movement.

Jennie shook herself mentally. Aiden was not looking for a relationship, and neither was she. They were simply friends. The truth of the matter was, neither knew the other. They'd only recently met. She'd lost track of time with how busy it was at the store but she knew it wasn't even a week.

It wasn't long and the kindling was alight. Soon the logs had caught fire, and heat filled the room. She sat on the edge of a lounge chair and indicated for Aiden to join her. "Coffee?" she asked. "Or have you had your fill?" She laughed then.

Jennie surprised herself. She was heartbroken over Nelson's disappearance, and here she was laughing. Enjoying herself.

She had no right to feel this way.

After ensuring the fire was well alight and burning nicely, Aiden came over and sat in a nearby chair. "It's a lovely place you have here," he told her, his voice gentle.

Jennie understood the reason for his words—he was being respectful of her grandparents, since it was originally their home. "It is beautiful, and I love it here. Except it's not made for one person." She closed her eyes for only a moment. "It feels far too empty without Nelson here."

Aiden reached across and covered her hand with his. This time it was skin-to-skin, since they had discarded their gloves. A thrill went up her arm. At first it alarmed Jennie. She had not experienced such a thing before.

Deep down, she knew exactly what was going on. She had grown attached to Aiden, even over this short period of time.

She needed to keep her distance, but the truth was, Jennie didn't want to. She felt something for Aiden. She wasn't sure what it was exactly, but there was a glimmer of something new and fresh when she was around him.

Right now, though, she had to focus her attention on finding Nelson. Jennie was certain he hadn't run out the door of his own accord. Why would he do so, when he'd never done it before?

He hadn't even attempted to run away before. None of it made any sense.

"Are you going to be alright by yourself?" Aiden was already standing up. It was clear he was ready to leave.

Jennie's heart thudded. She knew she had to stay here by herself tonight but hadn't wanted to think about it. She had no choice—Aiden had to go home, he had to look after Molly. He couldn't leave her alone all night.

When she looked into his face, he appeared conflicted. "I'll be fine, I promise," she said, trying to keep her voice even. The last thing she wanted was to make him feel guilty for leaving.

As though he could read her mind, Aiden shrugged his shoulders. "I would stay, except Molly..."

Jennie understood and told him so. "Of course you have to look after Molly. She is your priority. Besides, I will be fine by myself." Jennie knew her words were untrue. Aiden probably did too, but neither of them wanted to confess she needed him here.

It was then he stood and pulled his coat back on and reached for his gloves. He prepared himself to go out in the heavy snow again. Jennie felt bad sending him out there, when he could have already been home, in his own lounge room, near his own fire.

She also knew it had been his choice to accompany her here. She surely would have been fine walking home by herself, except tonight she didn't want to. Aiden's offer was just what she needed, at just the right time.

Walking to the door with him, Jennie felt terrible sending him out into the storm. The wind was picking up again.

Opening the door, she expected to see Nelson standing there, which she knew was not reasonable. He was a young dog, not used to the cold. He didn't even know his way home.

Did that mean if he escaped from wherever he was, he would get lost trying to find his way back to her? Jennie's heart thudded again. No matter which way she looked at it, Jennie was convinced she would never see Nelson again.

Chapter Twelve

Aiden hurried out the door before he changed his mind. He glanced skyward. The snow seemed to be heavier than before and the wind much stronger. Thankfully he didn't have much further to go to get to his own home.

Molly would be waiting for him, but Aiden knew she wouldn't be distressed. It was nothing new for him to be home late, he'd done it so many times before. Especially when they'd lived in the city.

He adopted Molly not long after the accident. She was what he needed, and Aiden was sure she needed him as well. Her elderly owner had died, leaving her homeless. He'd had a call telling him about Molly. At first, he rejected the offer, because none of this was about him. Except he finally realized it was about Molly and not for him alone.

Molly was a fully trained therapy dog, and he soon discovered she had not reached her potential. In the city, he volunteered at a clinic for the homeless, and believed Molly could help a lot of people there.

He was surprised at how quickly she settled in, and the difference she made to the patients there. He had mixed emotions about going to Pleasant Valley because of the clinic. But staying in the city meant living with the ghosts of the past.

It was simply unfortunate he had a contract he needed to fulfill at the hospital. They had the option to let him go, but the lack of available doctors led them to deny his early contract termination.

Aiden let out a sigh. He hated when thoughts rolled around his head like this. It was depressing, as if Nelson being missing wasn't depressing enough. He was relieved when he reached his home, and quickly unlocked the door. He opened it slightly, making sure Molly wouldn't escape into the chilly snow. Instead, she was relaxing in her dog bed, relishing the warmth from the central heating.

Aiden headed straight for the kitchen and prepared Molly's food. It didn't take her long to come for her food. He reached out and patted her head. "You're a good girl, Molly," he said. What he would do without her, Aiden did not know. They'd been together for a couple of years now and Molly had certainly earned her keep.

"It's time for you to get another haircut, but the weather is too cold. I'll bet you're happy with that," he said. Molly was always amenable at the groomer's, but there were some clear signs she preferred not to have her fur cut. Or a bath. Or her nails cut. It became apparent when she was put in the dog carrier and taken out to the car.

The silly thing was, she was always excited when she arrived. She didn't even care that he'd left her there. It was like Aiden no longer existed.

He watched as she gobbled up every last piece of her food. It wasn't so much that Molly was hungry, she was simply a dog that ate fast. Once she'd finished eating, she took a drink of water, then headed to her litter box. Aiden sat down on the comfortable chair in his lounge room. The heat that came from the fire at Jennie's place was comforting. Central heating was a whole different thing. Yes, it was warm, and it was comfortable throughout the house. It simply wasn't the same.

He thought about that for a moment. Was that because of the fire, or was it the company he kept? Aiden didn't want to know. Since the accident, he had kept to himself. He decided long ago it was the best thing to do. But now, here he was in a new town, making new friends. He felt it was best they remain ignorant of his past.

Without warning, Molly jumped up onto his lap. She might be a therapy dog for everybody else, but sometimes he needed her, too. Right now, this very moment, was one of those times.

If the weather wasn't so bad, and the wind as strong as it was, Aiden wouldn't hesitate to wrap Molly in a blanket and head back to Jennie. He was certain his best friend would brighten her day.

Until they had to leave. Which was inevitable. Then they'd have to trudge through the snow all over again. He couldn't do that to Molly.

Come to think of it, doing so wouldn't be fair to Jennie, either. It wasn't like he could leave Molly there. Not in a strange place, and without the one person she knew – Aiden. He shook himself mentally.

It was merely an idea. He processed it, judged and rejected it.

Aiden glanced at his watch. It was getting late, and he needed to eat. He had a busy day tomorrow, with both the clinic, and his own personal agenda. Worrying about Nelson weighed heavy on his shoulders.

He glanced down at Molly. Jennie would be missing Nelson. He would probably be on her lap by now. On a normal evening, that was. Sadly, not tonight.

Hers was a dilemma he wasn't sure could be solved. He worried Jennie may never see Nelson again.

Someone must have seen the abduction. It wasn't as though Nelson was hidden away from customers in the store. He was there in clear view. Right in the middle of the store where everyone could see him.

There was something he was missing, but Aiden couldn't fathom what that might be. He had to admit, even if only to himself, he was too tired and stressed to come to some sort of conclusion tonight. He knew the answer was there but couldn't process it in his current state.

For now, he would sit here with Molly. It would do them both good.

~*~

Morning came too soon, but at least he was able to sleep in. Even if it was only an additional thirty minutes.

Molly lay next to him in the bed, despite having her own luxurious bed. It was often this way – she would start off in her bed, then sneak into Aiden's bedroom in the early hours of the morning. He wasn't sure when exactly. Only a CCTV camera would give him that information.

That's when it hit him, the ideas that had been on the tip of his tongue all this time. He would have to talk to Jennie before making any decisions, and thankfully he had time this morning.

He showered and dressed then fed Molly. He decided to have breakfast at the café this morning. Perhaps he might even take Molly with him, she was good at comforting people when they needed it.

And there was no doubting Jennie needed comforting. Aiden wondered how she'd slept last night. Probably not at all well, due to the circumstances. Not that he'd slept much better. In the short time he'd known Nelson, he'd come to love the pup. Nelson was quite adorable, and everybody loved him. It simply did not make sense that he had been stolen. Kidnapped right out from under the eyes of everyone in the store at the time.

Aiden rugged up. It would be cold outside, considering the snow was no lighter now than it was last night. "Molly," he called. "Do you feel like going out with me?" He didn't have to ask twice, which was not surprising. Molly was at his feet in seconds.

This could go one of two ways—Molly could end up comforting Jennie over her missing dog, or Molly's presence could upset Jennie even more than she was now. He had to take the risk, and hoped the first option was the one that worked.

Chapter Thirteen

Jennie dreaded going to work. She had barely slept last night, which didn't surprise her in the least.

Although he had his own bed, Nelson often slept on her bed, and Jennie had really missed his nearness. She tried to do everything as normal, but it had proven difficult. After she'd showered and dressed, she began to go about her normal day.

The day always began with cuddling then feeding Nelson. She really missed that this morning. Jennie slumped down onto the sofa. She was heartbroken and the only thing that would fix that was for Nelson to come home.

She was convinced it wouldn't happen anytime soon. Hugging a cup of tea, Jennie knew she couldn't sit here all day. The sooner she got to work, the sooner she would stop feeling sorry for herself. There was plenty for her to do there, and keep her mind occupied.

She'd called most of the customers on the list last night. Unfortunately, none of them had seen anything untoward. There were still more people to call, and the best she could do was hold out hope that one of them saw something significant.

Jennie quickly finished her tea and pulled on her coat. The moment she was rugged up and ready to step out into the chilly winter weather, she did. At no point did she expect to bump into Aiden. But that was exactly what she did—he was waiting at the door to the bookstore when she arrived.

"Good morning," she said, shouting above the noise of the wind. Jennie unlocked the door and they went inside. Todd was already there preparing for the breakfast crowd. He began work far earlier than Jennie would ever contemplate.

When they were both inside, she locked the door behind them. It was far too early to let customers inside. Although if anyone was out there in this weather, she would let them in. There was no doubt about it.

The moment they were inside, Aiden opened his coat. A little head popped up. Jennie squealed with excitement. "This must be Molly," she said her voice full of excitement. "Can I pet her?" She would never assume it was alright to touch someone else's dog. Although she had allowed that to happen to Nelson. Jennie was now rethinking that strategy because of what had resulted.

"You can let her loose," Jennie said, excitement still in her voice. "Is she okay with the fire?"

Aiden nodded. "We had an open fire at our previous house." He didn't elaborate, and Jennie had no intention of prying. It didn't take long, and Molly had situated herself near the fire.

"She's a sweet thing," Jennie said. Despite her efforts to be cheerful, her sadness was evident. There was little she could do about it. Her best friend was kidnapped and still missing.

Todd greeted the pair at their table in the café. "Good morning to you both. Omelets are on the menu this morning," he announced.

"Yes, please!" Both Aiden and Jennie responded in unison. They glanced at each other and laughed. Todd stared at the pair, then strode into his kitchen.

It wasn't long before he returned with three coffees, which he placed on the table. He disappeared once again, and came back only minutes later, carrying three freshly made omelets. Todd placed one in front of each person, then sat down. Apart from Jennie and Aiden offering their thanks, not a word was spoken.

Jennie could feel the tension in the air, but was convinced this wasn't about Nelson's disappearance.

"That was delicious," Jennie said when she had finished eating.

Aiden wiped his lips with a napkin. "It certainly was," he added. "It's no wonder you have a thriving business here," he told Todd. "If only there'd been a café like this one back home."

Jennie glanced at her watch. "I have just enough time to freshen up and prepare the store for the day. She hurried off before anyone could respond. The last thing she wanted was to discuss Nelson. Her heart was already broken. She didn't need a reminder that her beautiful boy was absent.

As she left the café, Jennie spotted Molly. She was still positioned close to the fire and seemed content. The cavoodle lifted her head as Jennie approached her. Then she jumped up and waited for Jennie to get closer. Her tail wagged at a hundred miles an hour.

Jennie told herself she didn't have time to spend with Molly. Regardless of her belief, she settled down nearby. Close enough she could pet Molly, and not feel rushed. At first, she felt as though she was betraying Nelson.

He was not here, which was not his fault. Nor was it Jennie's fault. And it certainly wasn't Molly's.

As she sat with Molly, she found herself relaxing. Not as much as she normally was when Nelson was here, but better than she'd been since he disappeared.

She reached down and put her arms around Molly. The pair had a long, drawn out cuddle. She often did this with Nelson. It was one of his most favorite things to do.

"Molly loves cuddles." Aiden's voice startled her, and Jennie dropped her arms to her side. Guilt overwhelmed her. "Don't stop on my account," he told her, but Jennie felt the moment was over. Besides, she had work to do.

She glanced at her watch again. Fifteen minutes and the store would open. "I…I have things to do before the store opens," she said firmly. "Thank you for bringing Molly." The therapy dog's head shot up at her name being used. Jennie glanced down at her. She was such a sweet thing, and she couldn't help but bend down and pet her again.

"Molly will take that all day," Aiden told her.

Jennie was certain she would. Nelson was the same – the more pets he got, and the more attention, he wanted it to go on forever. The mere thought of Nelson being missing and what he might be enduring, broke her heart. What if she never found him? If she never saw Nelson again? And never got to hold him once more?

Her eyes filled with tears at the thought that it might happen. Jennie resolved not to weep and reached for Molly once more. As though she sensed Jennie's distress, Molly tried to jump up onto her lap. It was impossible for this small girl. Instead, Jennie picked her up and held her close.

Aiden walked away, leaving the two alone. She had never thought much about therapy dogs before, but now she understood. They were very special, and somehow, they comforted the person they were with. Whoever that might be at any given time.

Chapter Fourteen

The moment Aiden noticed her eyes brimming with tears, he walked away. Molly was doing exactly what she was trained to do. She was giving comfort.

He glanced at his watch. There was still time before the store was due to open. Jennie normally swept the floor before she opened up for the day. He figured he'd find a broom in the storeroom, so headed there.

As he thought, a wide broom stood against a shelf, just waiting to do what it was designed to do. He swept through the aisles of the bookshelves, then worked his way to the front door. Aiden was surprised how dirty the floors actually were. They didn't look that bad, and yet they were.

He swept up the large pile of dirt with a small broom and dustpan, then moved to the storeroom again. Wondering what else he could do to help, Aiden decided he probably shouldn't push his luck.

Already, he knew Jennie was an independent woman. She had her moments of weakness, especially when it came to Nelson. But overall, she relied on no one. His wife had been like that. It wasn't always the best thing, but it wasn't something you could stop.

By the time he'd returned to the front of the store again, Jennie was standing with the door open, greeting her customers. He stood back and waited until she was available. "If you want to go and freshen up, I can…" Aiden didn't get to finish the sentence.

"I'm fine," she interrupted. Then went to sit behind the counter. "Don't you have a clinic to attend?" It made him believe she wanted him gone.

Aiden knew she was probably right. "You are a cruel woman," he said, his words mocking. "Sending me out in the cold and the snow." Nonetheless, he retrieved his coat and gloves and put them on. "I'll see you soon," he said, sweeping Molly up into his arms, and concealing her inside his coat. The pair then hurried outside.

As he knew it would be, it was icy outside. He hugged Molly close to his chest. In normal circumstances, he would not have brought her along with him. Exposing her to this inclement weather, was not something he did lightly.

Jennie needed this, and they both knew it. For Molly, it was just another day at the office. She enjoyed meeting new people. She'd been trained for it and adored it. Much like most dogs. It was a trait know to cavoodles, and Molly was no different.

She was high maintenance, like other similar breeds. Brushing her each night proved beneficial to both Molly and Aiden. He would never allow her hair to become matted. It was not only an eyesore, it was painful for the dog. The time for her to be groomed was approaching. Molly loved her new groomer, which was not surprising. She loved everyone.

As the wind picked up, he hastened to reach his office. The cold weather was bearable, but only just. Aiden admonished himself for not putting Molly's warm jacket on her before leaving home today.

Exposing her to the elements was not his plan. Exposing Jennie to Molly was what he had in mind. At least Aiden knew she had helped his new friend. Even a short burst of exposure to the therapy dog was better than no time at all.

"Good morning."

Less than two minutes after Aiden had left the bookstore, he was surprised at the greeting. He glanced up and was surprised to see Mrs. Featherall tackling the wind and the snow. She held the large bag she always carried with her. "Good morning," he said tentatively. "What are you doing out in this dreadful weather? Could it not wait until the wind died down?" He was truly worried for the elderly woman.

She was not his responsibility, not really. Except Aiden had bought her husband's practice, and promised to look out for his wife after Ron Featherall was gone.

Harriet Featherall shook her head. "Oh no," she shouted to make herself heard. "This needs to be done immediately."

Aiden offered to escort her wherever she was headed. If it made him late for the clinic, so be it. Mrs. Featherall's well-being was far more important.

"I am perfectly fine," she said firmly, then hurried on her way.

Whatever it was, it was clear she was determined to do it alone. Ron had warned him she was likely to refuse any sort of help he might offer. He watched as Mrs. Featherall headed toward the bookstore, then hurried inside.

Relieved she had arrived safely, he continued to his own destination. It wouldn't be long before his first patient of the day arrived.

~*~

The moment he stepped inside the clinic, Aiden removed Molly from inside his coat. She was not at all concerned and scurried about the waiting room to visit her human friends. Aiden couldn't help but beam at the delight on his patient's faces.

Molly was such a sweet girl, and everyone loved her. Including Aiden. She had got him through a lot.

"Apologies for the delay, everyone," he said, as he approached Hannah's desk. She handed Aiden his patient list for the day, then called his first patient. "Mr. Smith," he said, then turned to Molly. "Come on, girl," he said quietly, and she ran into the consulting room without looking back.

"Mornin' Doc," George Smith told him. The elderly man looked far happier and much more relaxed today. "I just came to thank you for pushing me into getting a dog. She is a sweetheart."

Aiden couldn't help but smile. "Which one did you end up adopting?" He was pretty sure he knew which dog Mr. Smith would choose, but he was still undecided when Aiden left him a couple of days ago.

"I chose Winnie, the ten-year-old Jack Russell. I know I won't have her long, but then we might both fall off the perch in a few years." Aiden could hear the emotion in the old man's voice. "She deserves to live out her last years in a loving home, not a shelter."

"And now she will," Aiden said, feeling a little emotional himself. "Winnie may not be a therapy dog, but she is exactly what you need." He checked his patient's blood pressure while they chatted and was pleased to see it far lower. Which was not surprising.

Mr. Smith stood. "We need each other," he said, then strolled out the door.

Aiden was pleased to have helped. The welfare of his patients was paramount. Helping a patient choose a dog to see out their days was far better than filling them with medications that were not necessary.

Chapter Fifteen

Jennie waited near the fire as the book club ladies made their way into the café. Todd would have their usual table reserved, and their pastries would be ready and waiting for them. She wasn't sure which book they'd chosen to read and discuss this week, but she'd come to learn it didn't matter.

This book club was not about the books – it was more about a group of lonely women getting together once a week for a coffee, pastries, and a natter.

She was more than grateful to Aiden for helping her out earlier this morning. He swept the floors while she indulged herself in Molly's company. She had always had comfort from Nelson, but until now, she had no idea how much peace he brought to her.

Molly had filled the gap. For now. She hoped and prayed Nelson would be returned soon. Why he disappeared was beyond comprehension, but provided he was returned safe and sound, Jennie didn't care.

She only hoped his kidnapper had taken good care of him. She couldn't bear to think of sweet Nelson being mistreated. The very thought of it shattered her heart.

Todd served coffee to the book club table, and Jennie knew it was time for her part of the meeting. She hurried over and stood at the end of the large table. "Good morning, ladies," she said cheerfully, although it was farthest from how she felt. "Welcome to book club. Have fun discussing your book this week and enjoy your morning tea."

All six ladies began to speak at once. Jennie took that moment to make her exit. At the back of the store, there was already a number of people perusing the shelves. She would make her way there and check supplies. It wouldn't do to have gaps, especially in the children's section where she sold the most books this time of year.

After checking what she needed, Jennie headed to the storeroom. She collected up the books required, then refilled the stock. Her eyes scanned the room as she returned to the front of the store.

Her heart pounded. It…it couldn't be. Could it? She almost ran to the front of the store. There in his bed was her beloved Nelson. Tears filled her eyes, but this time Jennie didn't try to hold them back.

The moment she was near, Jennie snatched him up. Nelson seemed excited to see her, and his little tongue licked her hands and her face. Jennie had never been so relieved in her life.

Holding Nelson close to her chest, Jennie did not want to let him go but knew she must. She glanced about. Despite her elation at his return, the question on her lips remained – who had taken Nelson, and was that person here now?

In the café were the usual book club ladies. A few strangers sat drinking coffee, but she immediately discounted them. Strangers, that is, those who had never stepped inside the building before, had no opportunity to take Nelson.

At the bookshelves were the usual locals, and a handful of strangers. No doubt, tourists passing through. She could see Mrs. Peterson, Mrs. Spence, Mrs. Kramer, and a handful of other locals.

Her heart pounded. Nelson was back, but would he disappear again? He seemed unscathed despite his curious disappearance, but nonetheless, she wouldn't risk his being taken again. Jennie went behind the counter and placed him in the enclosed area she had for him there.

This could not happen again. Jennie promised herself she would not let Nelson out of her sight again. Not ever.

The moment he was settled, she reached for her cell phone. "Nelson's back." Saying the words out loud had her feeling emotional again. On the other end of the line came silence. For about five seconds.

"He's back?" Why she called Aiden of all people, she had no idea. Except he had helped her when she needed it most. He was a friend of the Featherall's and was the town doctor. He was a man to trust.

"How…?" The question seemed somehow unreal. As though he couldn't believe Nelson was truly back where he belonged.

"He was just there. It's book club day," she said, as though he should know what that meant. "I went about my work, and when I returned, he was there."

Even to her own mind, none of this seemed real. She was still trying to accept Nelson was gone. Now he was back, and Jennie wasn't sure it was even real. The entire situation was surreal.

"I can't come now, but once my morning list is finished, I'll be there," he told her. Aiden's words were comforting. Jennie had no idea why she felt different around him, but she did. Perhaps it was because Ron Featherall had trusted him. A friend of the family for many years, according to Aiden.

That was enough to satisfy any concerns she might have about him. When she ended the call, Jennie stared at Nelson. She still couldn't believe he had been returned, and for a moment, believed she was dreaming.

~*~

With only a few days until Christmas, the store was busier than ever. Jennie was loathe to leave Nelson alone, but she had little choice. With the amount of books being sold, she had no doubt the shelves were looking empty and forlorn.

They needed to be refilled.

Except Jennie was afraid to leave Nelson. Mulling over what she would do about this untenable situation, the door opened. A young woman hurried inside, followed by Aiden. The pair stomped their feet, then hung their coats on the rack at the door.

Aiden glanced up and smiled.

No, it was more than a smile. He grinned. Clearly, he was as happy as Jennie was to know Nelson was back. He rushed over to the counter, and the young woman followed. "Hear me out," he told her before uttering another word. "This is Claire. My practice manager's sister." He let the words hang, and it took a moment but finally Jennie got the connection.

She let out a long-needed sigh. It wasn't one of despair, but one that signaled to Jennie this was exactly what she needed. "You've worked in retail before?" she asked, feeling somewhat mean to have even asked the question.

"Not in a bookstore, but most recently in the sweet shop down the road. I have a resume." Claire offered Jennie the printed resume, so she supposed she should do the right thing and take it. As she scanned the details, she felt two sets of eyes on her. It took all her effort not to squirm.

A small bark pulled her attention away from the resume in her hands. "When can you start?" she asked, hoping it would be sooner than later.

"Now?" Claire answered. "Otherwise, whenever it suits you."

"Now is perfect," Jennie said in a rush. She moved her attention to Aiden. "Thank you. I've been talking about this for months. Since…" Her voice broke then. She couldn't say the words. *Since Grammy died.*

Aiden would know. He seemed to be able to read her mind.

"Can I hold him? It doesn't seem real." She knew exactly what Aiden meant. She glanced down at Nelson, then reached in and picked him up. He gave a little bark.

"He might need to go potty," she said apologetically.

Aiden reached across and took the sweet boy from her hands. "I can take him. Don't you worry."

Jennie nodded, then turned her attention to her new assistant.

Chapter Sixteen

Aiden held the small dog carefully. After everything he'd been through, Nelson may be injured. He wasn't a veterinarian, but he could check for surface injuries. First though, he would take the pup into the small garage to do his business.

Bringing Claire to the bookstore without Jennie's permission was bold. He knew she'd put it off for far too long, and desperately needed help. Hannah happened to mention her sister was looking for work, and did he know anyone.

He jumped at the opportunity and brought her here the moment she was available. Being Saturday, his clinic was a short one. The rest of the day was his to do whatever he pleased.

As he stood back and waited for Nelson to do his business, Aiden mulled over the situation. The biggest question in his mind was why anyone would kidnap a dog then return it. The entire scenario simply didn't make sense.

There appeared to be no advantage to anyone doing such a thing. Nelson climbed out of his litter tray and headed toward Aiden. Was he traumatized? It was difficult to tell, but he went straight to Aiden, who picked the pup up and petted him. "You're safe now, boy," he told Nelson.

But what if he wasn't? Nelson had been missing for less than twenty-four hours. There were no clues left behind indicating who had taken him. The kidnapper disappeared with Nelson without anyone seeing it occur.

Aiden took the opportunity to gently run his hands over Nelson. He checked the dog's paws and did his best to check in his mouth. He seemed to be in perfect health. Relief flooded him. He may not have known Jennie and Nelson for long, but already he had an affinity with the pair. There was a connection between them he'd not felt in a very long time.

As he carried Nelson through the bookstore to return him to Jennie, the ladies from the book club surrounded him, along with a few other customers.

"I'm so glad to see him back," one woman said.

Another reached out a hand and petted the pup. "It is such a relief."

He had to pull Nelson closer and protect him as the dog was becoming agitated. This was especially true when Mrs. Featherall approached him. "Misty," she said, her hand getting ever closer to Nelson. "It's time to go home."

At first Aiden was confused. "Misty?" he repeated.

Mrs. Baker approached Aiden and whispered in his ear. "Misty was Harriet's dog. She died of old age a couple of months ago."

It was all becoming clear. "This isn't Misty," Aiden told Mrs. Featherall firmly. "This dog is Nelson. He was Bridget Carpenter's dog."

The shocked look on Mrs. Featherall's face told him a lot.

Deidre Baker put an arm around the older woman. "It's all right, Harriet," she said gently. "I'll walk you home." Aiden watched as the pair moved away. They donned their coats and gloves, then headed outside into the chilly winter weather.

Now the mystery had been solved. Or at least Aiden thought it had, he wasn't sure of the next steps. Would he be able to convince Jennie? She seemed to have a special bond with the older woman. Which was understandable since her grandmother and Harriet Featherall were best friends for much of their lives.

"What do we do now?" he asked Nelson. The pup barked, then snuggled into Aiden's shoulder where he knew he was safe.

Now to tell Jennie. He wasn't sure how she would react, but hoped this would be the end of Nelson's adventures.

~*~

The closer Aiden got to the counter, the more nervous he became. He didn't want to be the one to break the news, but who else was going to do it?

Jennie was busy training Claire, and didn't want to disturb her. Except he knew he had to face the situation straight on.

She smiled as he approached her, Nelson snuggling into his chest. Claire was learning how the book shop operated and the register worked. Despite having worked in a retail store before, every register was different.

A customer stood in front of the counter, and Claire rang up her purchases, wrapped, then bagged them. "Thank you for visiting today," she said as the customer headed outside.

"That's a nice touch," Jennie told her when the customer was gone. "We might have to adopt it."

Claire turned to face her. "It's what we always said at the candy store," she said.

"I hate to interrupt," Aiden told the pair as he handed Nelson back to his rightful owner. "I have some information about Nelson's kidnapping," he said bluntly.

Both women stared at him.

Chapter Seventeen

Jennie couldn't believe what Aiden was saying.

Sweet, gentle, Mrs. Featherall had kidnapped Nelson? She had to admit Mrs. Featherall had seemed rather confused lately. Except she wouldn't hurt a fly. Why would she take Nelson?

Aiden continued to explain. "Nelson is apparently the same color as her deceased dog Misty. Was she the same breed?"

"I didn't know Misty had passed," she said, incredulous. "She was white like Nelson, but far bigger as she was older. Grammy chose Nelson because Misty had a sweet nature and was a quiet dog." She shook her head in disbelief. "How could this happen? She has known Nelson since Grammy got him from the shelter."

Another customer came to the counter, and the pair moved away. Jennie knew Claire was more than capable of looking after the customers. Besides, she would ask for help if it was needed.

She stared down into Nelson's face. The pup was adorable, and she could totally understand how Mrs. Featherall would want to keep him. Except she couldn't have him. Jennie couldn't bear to part with him. "I…I can't give him away. It's not what Grammy would want," she said, her voice breaking with each word spoken.

Aiden frowned. "I'm not suggesting you do. It won't solve the problem. I'm 99.9% certain it was Mrs. Featherall. I doubt we'll ever prove it, but it would be better to know for sure. There are things I can do to help her. And, of course, I will."

Jennie nodded. She was afraid if she tried to answer her emotions would come flooding out. Nelson was like a child to her, and he was her entire world. Grammy would have understood, and she was beginning to understand Aiden did, too.

"If you're happy to leave him here with Claire, we'll go to the café. You need to sit and take it all in."

She knew he was right. It was a bit much to cope with all at once. Normally she was fiercely independent, but today Jennie allowed Aiden to guide her to a table near the fire. It was always comforting sitting close to the flames. Especially on a day as cold as this one.

Todd wandered over before they were settled. His expression was one of doom. "Is everything alright?" he asked gently.

"It appears Mrs. Featherall is our dognapper," Aiden told him. "Jennie needs time to take it all in."

Glancing up at Todd, Jennie was shell-shocked. She had known the dear lady her entire life. Mrs. Featherall had babysat her as a small child. She even remembered the day Misty joined the Featherall family. To see the elderly woman like this was heartbreaking.

"She needs help," Jennie whispered, her voice breaking.

Aiden put an arm around her shoulders and pulled her close. "She does, and I'll ensure she gets it," he told her.

Jennie knew if Aiden said it, he would ensure it came to fruition.

~*~

A break from the busy store was what Jennie needed. Todd had pampered her and Aiden with cappuccino and pastries. She had allowed herself to indulge in the warmth of the fire, and the friendship Aiden had offered.

As they sat sipping coffee, he'd come up with an idea. He wasn't sure it was necessary now the culprit was found but decided it would work for any future mishaps.

He had left the store a short time ago, and she'd returned to training Claire. Nelson was safely, and happily, settled in his enclosure behind the counter.

"The storeroom is kept locked during opening hours," Jennie explained. "I don't want customers going in there and messing up the orderly manner of our excess stock."

"Of course," Claire told her. "Every store I've worked in has been the same."

Jennie studied her new employee for a moment. "If it's not a rude question, why did you leave those other jobs?"

Claire was silent, but only for a moment. "To them, I was just a spare. I never had regular hours, and they called when they needed help. Sometimes I had no notice whatsoever. It meant I couldn't plan anything."

Jennie couldn't believe what she was hearing. Who would treat people that way?

"The candy store wasn't like that," she added quickly. "I had set hours, but it was only casual. Nothing permanent."

"I've needed help for a long time. Well before my grandmother died." She paused to unlock the storeroom. "I've promised myself for months I would hire someone but never got around to it. Aiden ensured it happened."

"He's a great guy," Claire said. "My sister loves working for him, and I've met him several times before today."

"Molly is sweet, too," Jennie added. She adored Molly, which wasn't hard to do.

"I've stored the books in the same order they are in the store. What I generally do is check the shelves before the store opens in the morning. When it closes, it's time for coffee!" She smiled then, thinking about how Aiden had quickly become part of that scenario. "If you are happy to stay, you are invited to our little tea parties." She noticed Claire didn't react to her words. "You know this is permanent full-time, right?" Jennie asked. "That is, if you want to work with me."

"With you? Not for you?" Claire grinned. "I've waited to hear those words for a very long time. Of course, I'll stay – for as long as you want me."

After relocking the storeroom, they checked the shelves. Stocks were already depleted and needed replenishing. Jennie handed over her key to the storeroom. "You've got this," she told Claire. "I will get you a key of your own as a priority. In the meantime, I need to see to the customer at the counter," she said, then hurried to the front of the store.

This was exactly why she needed help. With Claire helping, it meant customers never had to wait to be served. "I'm sorry to keep you waiting, Mrs. Harper." Jennie rang up the customer's purchases and bagged them. "Merry Christmas to you," she said as her longtime customer headed toward the café.

She sat at the counter, her eyes scanning the store. It was then Jennie realized she was no longer anxious. For the first time in months, she was feeling relaxed.

It was soon afterwards Aiden came rushing through the door. He had two large bags in his hands, and a huge grin on his face.

Chapter Eighteen

Aiden placed the two bags on the floor while he removed his coat. He stomped on the heavy mat to loosen the snow.

Jennie stepped toward him. "Can I help?" she asked, glancing curiously into the bags.

He pulled the thick gloves off his hands as he shook his head. "Not this time. Unless…do you have a step ladder?"

She smiled. His heart fluttered.

Aiden knew he shouldn't, but he was falling for the bookstore owner. It had been two years. Actually, it was a little more, but that wasn't the point.

"I do have a step ladder," she said. "I'll go fetch it."

She was gone before he had a chance to tell her. Jennie deserved to know. And to hear it from him. Few people in town knew his story. Hannah did. Claire did, too, but neither were the type to gossip. Harriet Featherall was aware of his situation, but she was not in a position to recall much of anything.

He carried the two bags behind the counter. He removed his electric drill from one bag, and one of

the packages from the other. He then waited for Jennie to return.

She wasn't gone long – he was still testing the wall to find a stud where he could connect the CCTV. As he'd told Jennie earlier, it was too late in this instance, but if anything untoward happened in the future, the vision would be there for her to check.

She still appeared unsure. Had she decided not to go ahead? "Are we still doing this?" he asked gently. "You don't seem so sure."

"It's the noise I'm worried about," she told him quietly. "I don't want to disturb my customers." Of course. Why he didn't think of that himself, Aiden didn't know. He glanced at his watch. "Only another half hour and the store will be closed."

"Perfect." He packed up the supplies and placed them back in the bag, then put them underneath the counter and out of sight. "Is there anything else I can do to help in the meantime?" he asked.

Jennie shook her head. "Make yourself comfortable in the café?"

He could easily do that. Trouble was the fire would draw him in and tell him not to go back to work. Not that it was really work – Aiden enjoyed working with his hands. It was something he'd done when his wife…

Aiden shook himself mentally. "I'll just wander about," he said, and did exactly that.

~*~

He was at the back of the store when he noticed it. There was no movement, and the store was silent. He had listened to the low murmur of voices the entire time he'd been there, but now it stopped.

It meant only one thing – the store was now closed, and he could do the job he came back to do.

Making his way to the front of the store, his heart pounded. Aiden knew Jennie didn't really want this. She didn't want her customers to think she was spying on them. Except it wasn't like that. This was about protecting Nelson, and perhaps even her customers.

He had marked the wall earlier, so knew exactly where he needed to drill. He climbed up the stepladder and began work. He had also brought his smallest toolbox, and it sat on the counter in full view.

"What can I do to help?" Jennie asked him.

"Pass up that screwdriver and four of the screws I've laid out on the counter." It would save him climbing down again. "I've been thinking," he told her while he waited. "We need to find a senior dog for Mrs. Featherall. I believe that will solve the problem."

"One that looks like Misty?"

Jennie knew Misty and would be a big help finding a similar dog. "There are several seniors at the animal shelter. Provided it's still there, at least one dog fits the criteria." After drilling the holes high up on the wall, he reached down for the screws. "I'll put other services in place, so Mrs. Featherall gets to stay in her own home."

"Thank you," Jennie said, sounding genuine. "It means a lot to me, and I know it will to her."

Aiden climbed down from the stepladder. "That's one camera in place. Let's see where to place the others."

It didn't take long, and all three cameras were fitted and tested. It was time for coffee, and the three headed to the café.

"I was beginning to wonder if you were coming," Todd told them with a chuckle. "My coffee is too good to pass up, so I knew you'd get here eventually." He chuckled again. "What about you, Claire?"

"Coffee for me, please," she told him.

Aiden was pleased to see Claire had fitted in well. Jennie seemed to be happy, which was the most important thing. "How did your first day go?" he asked.

Before Claire had a chance to answer, Jennie jumped in. "Perfect, absolutely brilliant. Thank you for forcing me into action," she told him with a smile. "I would never have got around to it otherwise. Claire is amazing."

The coffee arrived then, and the aroma had him wanting to breathe it in. Only that would be rude. Todd placed a plate of pastries in the middle of the table and sat down to join them.

They chatted about the busy day they'd all had, then talked about the CCTV Aiden had installed.

"Let's hope it isn't needed again," Todd said.

"In regard to our dognapper, I predict it will not be necessary," Aiden told him. "Let's hope this is the end of a difficult time for Jennie, and for Nelson."

At the mention of his name, Nelson's ears perked up as he lay beside the fire.

Epilogue

Two days before Christmas

As the pair sat together in the café, Aiden turned to Jennie. "I must apologize," he said.

"For what?" she demanded. Aiden had never done anything to need an apology. She would know if it were the case.

He reached over and placed his hand over hers. "I should have told you before. Especially since our relationship has changed over the past weeks."

Jennie's heart pounded. What deep, dark secret was Aiden harboring? He didn't seem the type to do such a thing. She decided to stay silent and let him get whatever it was, off his chest.

He glanced down at the ring finger on his left hand. She followed his line of vision. "You're married," she said forcefully. Why had she not noticed the ring before?

"I was married. I'm a widower and have been for more than two years. My wife was killed by a drunk driver," he said. "I was one of the doctors on duty

in the ER when she was brought in. They wouldn't let me near her."

Did Aiden think it was his fault his wife had died? It was protocol, she was certain.

Jennie thought her heart would explode. She couldn't even begin to imagine such a scenario. She pulled her hands out from under his and clutched his hands tightly. "I'm so very sorry," she said. "I hope you don't blame yourself," she said gently. "Isn't it the law?"

He glanced up at her, his eyes swimming with unshed tears. "It is, but still…" He shrugged his shoulders then. "I know they did the right thing. Nothing would have saved her, and that's the truth of it."

Jennie desperately wanted to change the subject, if only to make Aiden feel better. "Mrs. Featherall seems to have settled into her new life. Thank you for everything you've done for her."

"I did the same for her as I did for one of my other patients." He took a sip of the coffee that sat untouched on the table. "This is what I love about small towns. Working in an ER, you fix the problem, then send the patient out into the world again. Unless they are extremely unlucky, you never see them again."

"That must be hard," Jennie said softly.

"It was. I don't ever want to do it again. Here, I get to spend time with my patients. I have Molly to assist me, and she helps a lot. I get to follow up on them and put services in place where necessary."

"Or organize senior dogs." She grinned. Aiden had done this twice now, and it had worked out beautifully for both patients.

"We don't know each other very well," Aiden said. "But I'd like to get to know you better. You and Nelson. Perhaps we can go out to dinner sometime."

Jennie squeezed his hands. She wanted to get to know the town doctor far better than she already knew him. She didn't hesitate. "How about tonight?" she said.

Aiden grinned.

From the Author

Thank you so much for reading my book – I hope you enjoyed it.

I would greatly appreciate you leaving a review on Amazon, even if it is only a one-liner. It helps to have my books more visible on Amazon!

About the Author

Multi-published, award-winning and bestselling author Cheryl Wright, former secretary, debt collector, account manager, writing coach, and shopping tour hostess, loves reading.

She writes historical romantic suspense and historical western romance, and cozy mysteries.

She lives in Melbourne, Australia, and is married with two adult children and has six grandchildren, and three great-grandchildren. She can be found in her craft room making greeting cards.

Links

Website: *http://www.cheryl-wright.com/*

Facebook Reader Group:
https://www.facebook.com/groups/cherylwrightaut hor/